# HIS REASON TO STAY

**CATHRYN FOX**

# COPYRIGHT

Discover other titles by Cathryn Fox at www.cathrynfox.com.
Please sign up for Cathryn's Newsletter for freebies, ebooks, news and contests:
https://app.mailerlite.com/webforms/landing/c1f8n1
ISBN 978-1-928056-60-7
Print ISBN 978-1-928056-77-5

# PROLOGUE

Rachel Andrews glanced at the clock, then turned her attention back to the patient in her chair. Christmas music filtered in through the speakers above as she grabbed the dental floss, and coiled it around anxious fingers. In two short hours she'd be picking James up at the airport and she was excited to have him home for the holidays. Truthfully, she hadn't seen much of him since he went off to Harvard right after their high school graduation two years ago. They might have started dating prom night, but she'd spent far more time with his younger brother, Kyle —before he enlisted in the army.

She continued with her cleaning, and thought about the two brothers who meant everything to her. After Rachel's dad had died of a massive heart attack, she and her mom had moved to Austin during Rachel's sophomore year. A friend had introduced her to James and she met Kyle through him. The three had instantly hit it off. They were all tight through high school, and in all honesty she loved both brothers equally. By the time their senior year came around, James became a little more possessive around her, and the two started dating before he went off to Harvard. A natural progression of their relationship, she supposed. While he was away, Rachel went to work at night to put herself through dental hygiene school, and Kyle, much to his parents' disappointment, joined the army the minute he was old enough. She wasn't sure why he wanted out of Austin so badly, only that he was eager to move away. God, she'd missed him so much, and when he upped and left after high school without so much as a goodbye, it nearly tore her apart.

Floss in hand, she swallowed down her emotions, finished the cleaning and straightened. "All set," she said. She removed the bib from around the woman's neck, and pressed a button to lift the chair. "Any plans for the rest of the day?" Rachel peeled off her gloves and tossed them onto the counter.

"Just finishing up some shopping."

Rachel groaned. She'd been so busy she hadn't even begun hers. Not that she had many people to buy for. Outside of her mother, the only family she had were James and Kyle. Not that the guys were related or anything. She and James had never even talked about a future. But they were both close to her heart and she'd be lost without them.

Her client stood, and Rachel walked her out to the front of the clinic. As she made her way to the counter to pay, Rachel hurried back to her station to clean it, ready to check out for the weekend. She said goodbye to the staff, grabbed her coat and rushed outside. She had just enough time to get home, shower, and change and make it to the airport on time.

The second she stepped outside and found Kyle leaning against his car waiting for her, her heart leapt. "Kyle," she squealed. She ran to him, and he picked her up, spinning her around as he hugged her tight. "What are you doing here?"

He grinned and set her back down, but kept his arms around her. "Oh, you know, just hanging out in front of the dentist's office because a guy never knows when he's going to chip a tooth."

Laughing, she hugged him tight, the warmth of his body chasing away the chill in the air. "I didn't even know you were home."

"Got back early."

"Your mom and dad must be excited to have the extra time with you." She fought off a shiver at the mention of his mom. No matter how hard she tried, she could never do anything right in Irene's eyes. Neither could Kyle.

"Haven't seen them yet."

Her heart gave a little start to know he'd come to see her first. God, how she'd missed him. His gaze moved over her face, then his eyes met hers. They held for an extra moment, then he let go of her and opened his car door.

"Get in. It's freezing out. I'll drive you home."

"I only live two blocks away." She slid into the car anyway, and he crossed the front and hopped in to the driver's seat. He grabbed the stick shift and she closed her hand over his. "James is getting in tonight. Will you be able to go to the airport with me? He'll be happy to see you."

He scoffed. "He's been gone for four months. It's not me he's going to be happy to see."

"Don't be crazy. Besides, I want you to come."

"I don't know, Rach."

Honest to God, she didn't want him out of her sight, for fear that he'd up and take off again. "Pleeeease...."

He smiled and shook his head. "You know I can never say no to you."

"Good." She relaxed into her seat as he pulled in to traffic and drove the short distance to the apartment she shared with her friend Sara, to cut costs.

He parked and they both darted up the stairs. Inside her small apartment, Kyle plunked himself down on her sofa and grabbed the remote. She glanced at him, noting how at home he seemed in her place. James hated her apartment. Said it was cramped and cluttered, but Kyle looked like he belonged.

"Give me a minue to shower and change." She darted down the hall, peeling her clothes off as she went. Twenty minutes later she emerged from her bedroom, wearing jeans and a sweater with a hint of makeup. Kyle climbed to his feet when he saw her and his glance moved down her body, a slow inspection that rippled through her blood.

Blue eyes locked back on hers and a muscle along his jaw ticked. "You look beautiful, Rach."

She laughed, but there was no humor in his eyes. "I bet you say that to all the girls."

"No just to you."

"Yeah, and the rest of the women you have falling at your feet." She wagged a finger at him. "I see how women look at you." He opened his mouth, like he wanted to say something, then shut it again. "Kyle?" she asked.

"We better get moving." He checked his watch. "Traffic is heavy."

She nodded, slipped on her boots and coat, and locked the door behind them. Kyle put his arm around her and offered his warmth when they stepped into the wind. Inside the car, she blasted the music and sang along to the Christmas carols. Kyle kept casting glances her way, grinning as she sang off tune. But she didn't care. She was happy. Her two favorite men were home, and that was the best Christmas present ever.

At the airport, Kyle parked and they dashed through the parking garage. She checked the board inside and clapped when she saw James's plane had arrived.

"Come on." She grabbed Kyle's hand. His big palm practically swallowed hers whole as she tugged him, maneuvering through the crowd until they reached the escalator. They stood at the bottom, and ten minutes later, she spotted James. His glance met hers and her heart beat faster when he gave her a big smile. That smile however, faltered a bit when he noticed his brother.

James reached them and she let go of Kyle's hand to give him a hug. He picked her up and spun her, in much the same manner as Kyle had earlier. His lips landed firmly on hers, kissing her possessively.

After a very public display of affection that made Rachel slightly uncomfortable, James put his hand on Kyle's shoulder. "Hey, little brother, good to see you."

"You too." Kyle threw his arms around James and gave him a hug. A noise sounded at the luggage carousel and Kyle inched back. "I'll grab your bag for you and give you two a minute." Rachel smiled. That was just like Kyle. Always watching out for his older brother and conscious of his needs. There wasn't anything Kyle wouldn't do for him.

As James pulled her in close, she cast a glance at Kyle, who suddenly couldn't seem to meet her eyes.

James shifted his backpack. "No need. I packed light. Let's get out of here." They started toward the car, Kyle walking a few feet ahead of them to give her and James a bit of privacy, she assumed. James leaned in to her. "I made reservations for us at Lucien's."

She blinked, surprised. Lucien's was a very expensive restaurant, and she was far from dressed properly. Not to mention a meal there probably cost more than she made in a day. "You did?"

"I wanted to go straight there."

Her brow furrowed. "You don't want to go home first?"

"No."

Rachel looked him over. He seemed anxious about something. "Is everything okay?"

"Yeah, I just didn't expect to see you with Kyle, and the reservation is for two."

"I asked him to come. Do you think we can change it to three?" She didn't want to leave Kyle out.

"Hey," Kyle said, slowing to let them catch up. "You two go ahead to dinner. I have things to do anyway."

She put her hand on his arm. "But I want you to come."

"Yeah, me too," James said. The brothers exchanged a look Rachel didn't understand.

"You sure?" Kyle asked.

"Yeah, I think you should come. You should be there."

Rachel wasn't sure what James meant by that, but she was happy that they were all going to be together. James pulled his phone from his pocket and called the restaurant as they made their way to the car.

The brothers sat in the front, catching up with one another, and Rachel claimed the back seat. She sat there grinning, her heart so full she was unable to wipe the smile from her face.

Thirty minutes later, they were led to a quiet table in the back of the restaurant, and James ordered a bottle of wine. As they sipped, his hand closed over hers, and across from her Kyle shifted in the seat.

"It's good to be home." James leaned in to press his lips to hers. This time she was the one shifting. Sure they were dating, but it felt oddly wrong kissing James in front of Kyle, and James seemed to be showing more affection in front of his brother than usual. His lips lingered and he coiled his fingers in her hair. "I missed you so much." Before she could answer, James pushed his chair back, and then he went down on one knee.

Rachel gasped and her gaze instantly shot to Kyle. He sat ramrod straight in his chair, his eyes locked on hers, his mouth set in a grim line.

"Rachel," James said, a note of irritation in his voice. "Look at me."

She turned her attention to James, her heart pounding so hard in her ears, she could barely hear anything.

He pulled a box from his pocket and tears pricked her eyes. Was this really happening? Here, in front of Kyle? Is this what he wanted his brother to see?

"Will you marry me?" he asked.

"Oh, my God," she said under her breath. Once again her gaze crept to Kyle's. The muscles along his jaw ticked, and his Adam's apple bobbed as he swallowed hard. Her throat tightened, her vision going a little fuzzy around the edges.

She blinked, and something in Kyle's face softened. There was a slight nod of his head as he pushed back in his seat. As he distanced himself both physically and emotionally, she turned back to James and knew she had her answer.

●<br>**1**

*T*wo *years later*

The prison sentence could very well be worth it.

Mouth agape, Rachel Andrews stood inside her soon-to-be in-laws' grand entranceway, her heart crashing against her chest as she listened to the words coming from her future mother-in-law's perfectly painted lips. Rachel was calm by nature, never one to rock the boat, but as she fisted her hands at her sides, blind rage filled her.

So did the need to strangle someone.

After bullying Rachel on every wedding detail—big and small—Irene Nelson was now trying to get her and James to change their honeymoon plans. Hell no! They'd planned the trip months ago. The tickets had been bought on a payment plan, the resort had been booked, and she was already packed, for God's sake.

Irene smoothed a strand of jet-black hair behind her ears, showcasing diamond earrings that were worth more than Rachel's monthly paycheck. The pretty, middle-aged woman dipped her head and looked down her nose at Rachel, continuing with, "I mean why go halfway across the world when we have a perfectly good cottage at Fox Point?"

Desperate to occupy her hands before she wrapped them around Irene's neck, Rachel briefly pinched the bridge of her nose, then darted a glance at James, who was rubbing his chin, a familiar habit when he was mulling something over. The pulse in Rachel's neck leapt. Surely to God he wasn't considering changing their honeymoon destination, wasn't going to let his mother strong arm him into doing what she wanted—again.

Hawaii was *his* idea.

"James," Rachel said through gritted teeth. He angled his head toward her, and when soft, translucent blue eyes met hers, Rachel's stomach dropped. She loved him, she truly did, but how could he not stand up for her, for them? Rachel sucked in a quick breath and opened her mouth, even though she wasn't sure what to say, but Irene was quick to cut her off anyway.

"An expensive honeymoon is a bit frivolous at this point, don't you think? You need to think about building wealth, not spending money you don't have yet. James has only begun his career at the investment firm." Irene steepled her hands in front of her chin, a breathy laugh shuddering past her lips as she looked heavenward. "I'm just glad James's father and I could help out with the wedding costs, since the bride's side wasn't...well, you know."

Wow. It took real skill to insult someone while flashing a million dollar smile.

"And you know we appreciate all you've done," Rachel began through clenched teeth, even though she hated the idea of them paying for anything. She'd wanted a small wedding, immediate family and a few close friends only. Those were the things important to her. But the Nelsons were determined to have a huge, elaborate affair, inviting all their influential friends. They insisted on throwing money at the event to give their oldest son the "royal" wedding he deserved.

Like they'd said to Rachel and James on numerous occasions—if it's worth doing, it's worth doing right. Clearly appearances were everything to the Nelsons. While Rachel didn't want anything to do with an extravagant wedding that was well beyond her budget, James had talked her in to accepting the gift, because it was what his mother wanted.

*What about what I want?*

A beat passed, and Rachel folded her arms and waited for James to say something...do something. When he continued to rub his chin, the rasping sound drilling on her very last nerve, Rachel spoke up. "Everything is already booked."

Irene waved a dismissive hand. "That's easy enough to change." James's mother blinked dark lashes over eyes that mirrored her son's. "James is just starting at the firm and hasn't established himself financially yet, and you, well..."

She let her voice fall off, leaving what she really wanted to say unspoken—James could do so much better than the girl from the wrong side of the tracks, one who didn't have the right job or pedigree to step into the Nelson family.

In all the time she spent with the guys, Irene had never once treated her like she was part of the family. Now here they stood, one month before the ceremony and Irene was still hell-bent on trying to drive a wedge between Rachel and her son.

"James," Rachel began, her blood burning.

He turned to her and reached for her hand. "You know, Rachel, she does have a point."

*What the hell!*

Without missing a beat Irene pounced. "That's right,

James. Mother does know best." She flashed a smile Rachel's way then turned back to James, but Rachel could see right through her. The woman was a wolf in sheep's clothes. Irene smoothed her hands over the collar of James's crisp white dress shirt and beamed with pride as she looked up at him. "I'll even make sure to stock the cottage with all your favorite foods."

Rachel practically vibrated as heat crawled up her neck. With her body shaking, her face undoubtedly the color of a tomato, and steam coming from her ears like she was ready to blow, she could only imagine how crazy she must look to them. James hated confrontation as much as she did, but he needed to stand tall and put a stop to his mother's interfering once and for all. Since it was his family, it was his place to do it, not hers. A strange strangled noise caught in her throat as she twisted her diamond engagement ring.

Irene angled her head. "Are you okay, dear?" Rachel swallowed, trying to find her voice. Although, even if it did resurface, she was sure she wouldn't be able to get the words past the lump in her throat. Irene patted James's shoulder, a triumphant look on her face, and inched back. "Perhaps I should give you two a minute."

Irene's heels clicked on the polished marble floor as she stepped into her library and closed the double doors behind her.

"You're kidding me, right?" Rachael whispered. "You're actually agreeing with her on this?"

"Come on, Rachel." James pulled her to him and brushed her hair from her shoulders. "She did pay for the wedding."

"That doesn't give her the right to have a say on everything we do, and you know I didn't want her to pay for it in the first place," she shot back. "This whole elaborate wedding is what she wants, not me."

Rachel broke from the circle of his arms, stepped back, and put her hand on her forehead. Would her entire marriage be like this? Irene manipulating her son and twisting things until she got what she wanted? When would James ever stand up to her? His whole life he'd done everything to please his folks, their approval being the most important thing in the world to him. *Maybe even more important than me.* That realization stopped her cold. Her stomach clenched, equal amounts of anger and sadness curdling her blood as that truth penetrated her soul.

"It will be fun at Fox Point." He shoved his hands into the pockets of his laundered beige khaki pants. "We can go swimming, boating, have a bonfire."

"We do those things every other weekend," she countered, her voice rising to the point of hysteria, despite the fact that she didn't want Irene to overhear their private conversation. But she couldn't help herself. What James did next was important in so many ways. "This is *our* honeymoon, James. The beginning of *our* future."

"This time it will be different at Fox Point, because we'll be married."

Her head started spinning. Did he really believe that?

"This isn't even about our honeymoon anymore," she shot back. "Don't you see? She'll never think I'm good enough for you." She drew in a breath and let it out slowly, her insides twisting as that truth settled in the pit of her stomach like a clump of cold oatmeal. "She doesn't want us married, James. She's trying to drive us apart."

He gave her a look that suggested she was crazy. "That's not what she's doing. She has our best interests at heart."

"She has *your* best interests at heart." She shook her head, her heart aching. "You didn't even stand up for me."

"What did you want me to do?" His voice turned hard as

he went on the defense. Good God, if he could hold his own against her, why the hell couldn't he do it with his mother?

"I wanted you to tell her you're a grown man and can make your own decisions. That Hawaii was your idea, and how much you've been looking forward to going. It's all you've been able to talk about."

"But she did have a good point." He smoothed a hand through his short hair. "We should be thinking about our future."

Heartache set her chest on fire. "You're right. We should be." She twisted her ring off, letting the decision settle in her brain. "And since you're always going to take her side over mine, you two can go to Fox Point and figure out what that future is." She threw the ring at him, and he flinched. The diamond clattered to the floor, and right on cue, his mother stepped back in to the foyer.

"Rachel, come on." James reached for her.

She dodged his hand and turned. Tears spilled down her face as she opened the front door and a burst of sunlight blinded her as she hurried outside. James started after her but Irene stopped him. The two exchanged words as Rachel ran down the stone walkway, not daring to look back. The last thing she wanted to see was his mother flashing her perfect white teeth in victory.

She hopped into her car and swatted at her tears as she turned the engine over and drove away. She sped through the street, having no idea where she was going until she drove past Sky Bar. When she spotted Kyle's motorcycle, the tears fell harder. She'd missed him so much when he was overseas. He'd taken leave and come home early for their wedding, to stand as James's best man, but he seemed to be making himself scarce. The engine sputtered as she shut down the car and hurried from the vehicle, desperate to talk to Kyle. He'd understand. Unlike James, he never needed his parents' approval and lived life the way he wanted.

The instant she pushed through the bar's heavy doors, he lifted his head like he could sense her presence long before he could see her. The second their eyes met in the dimly lit bar, he shoved his beer away and jumped from his chair so fast, he sent it flying backward. His comrades all turned to see what had caught his attention as he hurried toward her. Long legs made quick work of the distance as eyes identical to his brother's remained latched on hers. While the two guys were unnervingly similar, there was a toughness about Kyle, a thickness to his muscle and a hardness in his eyes that his brother lacked. Perhaps it was from his years spent overseas, or from opposing his folks for so long. The strain had to be hard on him. Either way, he wasn't a man who let anyone push him—or her—around.

"What's wrong?" He dragged her into his arms.

She sagged against his chest, taking comfort in the strength of his embrace. Her tears soaked his shirt as she breathed in his familiar scent—sand, sun, and beach on a warm summer day. She tried to talk, but her words came out garbled.

"Hey, Rach, come on." He ran his hands through her hair, a gentle touch that helped calm her nerves and chase the chill from her body. "What is it?"

"James," she said.

He stiffened, put both hands on the side of her head and pulled her from his chest. She tilted her head, and his eyes moved over her face. "What did he do?"

"Nothing." She choked out. "That's the problem."

He frowned, confusion backlighting his eyes. "You're not making sense."

"I left him," she said. "I gave back the ring. It's over."

Air left his lungs in a whoosh and washed over her cheeks as conflicting emotions flashed across his face. "Rach..." he began, his voice rough. "This is a mistake."

"He never stands up for me, Kyle. He's canceling our honeymoon plans because your mother doesn't think it's a good idea. Hawaii was *his* idea. She's always interfering, always making up his mind for him."

A spark of understanding moved over his eyes as his jaw seesawed from side to side. He pulled her back, and hugged her tighter, his heart thundering against her cheek.

"Okay, let's get out of here." He exchanged a look with his comrades then put his arm around the small of her back to lead her outside to her car. He kept her close, guiding her around the parked cars until they reached her driver's side.

He brushed her hair from her face, and looked her over, a careful assessment. "Are you okay to drive? I had a couple beers with the guys and I shouldn't be behind the wheel."

"Yeah," she said, her nerves much calmer than when she'd first arrived. Kyle always made everything better.

Kyle wiped the remaining tears from her cheeks, the pads of this thumbs rough against her skin. He dipped his head and she caught the sweet tang of beer. "Are you sure? If not I can call us a cab."

"I'm sure."

"Okay." He opened the door for her and she climbed in. His eyes remained locked on hers, worry lingering in their stormy depths as he crossed the front of the car and hopped in to the passenger side.

She sat there staring at the wheel. He put his hand on hers and she turned toward him. Her heart missed a beat. He'd been away too long.

He gave her hand a squeeze. "Where to?"

She didn't want to go back to the apartment she still

shared with Sara, and sitting in a coffee shop in the state she was in was out of the question. "The bluff, I guess."

She drove twenty minutes until she reached the spot where they all hung out in high school. They parked at the foot of the hill and hiked to the top, and she turned her face to the late-day sun, her thoughts a jumbled mess. Kyle put his hand on her cheek to gain her attention.

"Tell me what happened."

She leaned into his hand, and he drew her close until her body pressed against his. With her emotions in turmoil, she circled her hands around his waist and relaxed into his strength, taking comfort in him being there.

"It's over," she whispered, her hands splaying over his back, his hard muscles tightening beneath her touch. His breathing became a little more ragged and she listened to his throat work as he swallowed.

"You need to go back," he whispered, his voice so strained it was hard to understand him. "You two are meant for each other. You guys can work this out, Rach. I know you can."

She shook her head, her damp cheek brushing over his chest. "No, I'm not going back, not if he keeps letting your mother run our lives."

"I'll talk to her. I'll tell her to back off."

"You shouldn't have to, and it will cause more tension between you all anyway."

"I don't care. She has no right to interfere."

"It doesn't matter anymore. It's over."

"Rach..." he began, a note of desperation in his voice as it dropped an octave.

A moment passed, and he touched her chin, lifting her eyes to his, but it wasn't her eyes he was looking at. As he zeroed in on her mouth, he swiped his tongue over his bottom lip. He drew a ragged breath, the hand he had on her face shaking. Her insides trembled. There was nothing casual in the way he was looking at her. It stirred all the deeper emotions inside her. His eyes snapped shut, like he was waging some internal war, and when he opened them again, they were the deepest shade of blue she'd ever seen.

"Kyle," she began, but lost all train of thought when his lips came down over hers.

P*resent Day, five years later*

Air evacuated Kyle's lungs as he stood on the cracked and pitted sidewalk stealing glimpses of Rachel as she pushed her daughter, Ava, on the swing at Glenmore Community Park. The last time he'd seen them was a little over two years ago. Ava had only been a toddler when they'd buried her father.

Kyle's stomach clenched, never having gotten over the passing of his brother. As a military man he was used to death, but the loss of James had damn near killed him. His muscles tightened, flattening the gift bag he had in the crook of his arm as he gripped the chain-link fence surrounding the park. He squeezed the wire until his knuckles turned white, and sucked in a quick breath, desperate for air. Desperate to keep himself in check as he watched mother and daughter at play.

*Rachel.*

Jesus Christ he loved her so fucking much. His years on the battlefield did little to diminish his love for her, but she wasn't his—she never had been. He needed to remember that. They'd been so close years ago, but after she'd started dating his brother, and the two began down a path that didn't involve him, Kyle had no reason to stay in Austin. He'd upped and joined the army right out of high school, and began one of many tours overseas.

He'd only been home twice since James and Rachel had gotten engaged. Once for his brother's wedding. Once for his funeral. Both had been painful.

Rachel laughed as she pushed her daughter higher and higher, and as the sound wrapped around his soul his mind went back to the afternoon at the bluff—even though he'd long ago vowed never to think about it again.

He'd made a horrible mistake that day, one he'd never forgive himself for. Rachel wasn't in her right mind, and taking her into his arms and making love to her might have been the sweetest moment of his life, but he never should have given in to the things she'd aroused in him. Never should have let his weakness for her—or her emotional vulnerability at the time—overshadow sensibility. While he'd like to blame his lack of self-control on the beers he'd put back with the guys, that was pure bullshit and he knew it. Then again, he could also try to convince himself that she'd been split from his brother when she'd come to him, so *technically* they hadn't cheated. But that was nothing but a load of crap too.

He was a grown man, one who knew right from wrong, which was why immediately after making love to her, he'd tried to convince her to go back to James and work things out. The two belonged together. Of that he was sure. But she'd refused, cancelled the wedding and stopped taking James's calls, even though everyone knew she still loved him. But her future wasn't with Kyle, despite what had happened between them and he'd told her that. After another few weeks of reflection, and a lot of hard work and groveling on James's part, she'd come to realize what Kyle had always known—she belonged with James. Unlike Kyle, James was a great man, one with a bright future in front of him.

*James.*

Christ, he was the best older brother a guy could ever ask for. He was the world to Kyle, and Kyle would have done *anything* to make sure he received the parental approval he so desperately needed. He wasn't sure why James constantly needed their consent; perhaps it had something to do with being the first-born. Regardless, Kyle had always put James on a pedestal and stood in the shadows of his greatness for many years. In fact, he went to great lengths to ensure he stayed in those shadows during their youth. But that didn't stop the guilt of betrayal from eating his gut like a goddamn parasite, and now he was determined to prove himself an honorable man.

Rachel laughed at something Ava said, the sound seeping under his skin and touching his darkest corners. His heart squeezed. The last time he'd seen her she had the strain of loss written all over her face. Now here she was, finding some semblance of happiness as she picked up the pieces of her life.

As if sensing him there, her eyes lifted, and the smile fell from her face when their gazes collided. She went as still as a stealth soldier as the swing came back and hit her across her hip. Her hands grasped for air as she stumbled backward, and Kyle pushed though the chain-link gate and darted across the playground. He dodged dogs, small children, and strollers as they crossed his path, needing to get to her.

When he reached her, he found her flat out on the ground. He dropped to one knee and cupped her elbow. His thumb slid along her skin. Warm, silky soft, the way he remembered. His heart pumped faster than a military issue rifle, but it had little to do with his quick sprint across the park.

"Are you okay?" he asked.

"I…I…Kyle?" She blinked three times and stared at him, like she was trying to figure out whether he was a figment of her imagination or not.

"Yeah, it's me," he said softly. "I'm really here."

"What?" she whispered, her hair tangling beneath her as she shook her head. "When?"

He captured her hand and pulled her to her feet. His gaze left her face to look her over. "Are you hurt?"

"No." She wiped shaky hands over her shorts, brushing the grass from her clothes with a little more force than necessary. "I'm okay."

"Mommy?" a small voice asked.

"Ava." She scooped her daughter up on to her hip, and held her close. "Oh, honey, are you okay?"

Dressed in a frilly pink princess gown, Ava touched her mother's face with tiny fingers, a frown tugging down the corners of her mouth. "Mommy, why did you fall down?"

"I slipped. I'm okay. I promise," she said, her words coming out a little too fast. She was trying to present a calm demeanor, and actually might have succeeded with someone else. Someone who didn't know her as well as he did.

Coming to her rescue and giving her a moment to catch her breath and get herself under control, Kyle turned his focus to her daughter. "Hi, Ava. Do you remember me?"

Ava looked at Kyle and shook her head, her blonde curls bobbing around her face.

Rachel tugged on her daughter's dress, to smooth it over her knee. "This is Kyle. He's your…" She stopped speaking, and shifted from one foot to another.

Christ, he'd really thrown her off. He hadn't meant to. He thought stopping by instead of calling might ease the awkwardness of seeing each other again after all this time. He'd been wrong.

"I'm your uncle," he said.

Ava looked a bit unsure. "What's an uncle?"

Kyle laughed. "An uncle is a friend of your mom's who brings presents."

Blue eyes that mirrored her father's went wide and focused on the gift bag under his arm. She pointed a small finger. "Is that mine?"

He nodded and Ava squirmed until Rachel set her down. Rachel straightened and smoothed her hair back. Unable to help himself, he reached out and pulled a strand of grass from her hair.

"I must look a mess." She quickly, finger-combed her long, brown curls.

"You look fine, Rachel." As beautiful as ever, actually.

Her face turned a shade of pink that matched her daughter's dress, and she looked everywhere and anywhere but at him. As Ava stared at him, he handed her the gift bag.

"You didn't have to do that," Rachel said.

"I wanted to. Besides I have a lot of birthdays to make up for."

Ava took the bag. "Thank you," she said.

Kyle smiled at Rachel. "She's very polite. She must take after her uncle."

Rachel laughed. "I don't think politeness was ever your strong suit, Kyle. You mostly said what you wanted and did what you wanted. Don't you remember the fights you had with your parents?"

He rubbed the back of his neck. "Yeah, how could I forget?" Truth be told, Kyle might have been the younger sibling, but everyone considered him the golden child. Everything he did he excelled at. There wasn't a ball he couldn't catch, a bat he couldn't swing, or a touchdown he couldn't make. The teachers even wanted to bump him up a grade in school and place him in his brother's class. He couldn't allow that to happen, so he let his grades slide and dropped out of every sport his parents put him in. He constantly fought with his folks for not applying himself like James. But he didn't care. James was more important to him than their approval.

"How long are you home?" Rachel asked, dragging his thoughts back.

"Not long. I'll be here for Easter, and then I'll be shipping out."

She smiled, but he could tell it was forced. Did the sight of him remind her too much of James? Their betrayal at the bluff? Not that she was in any way responsible. She was in a fragile state of mind when she'd come to him, and he'd taken advantage of that. Fuck, how could he have been such a selfish bastard?

He kicked a small pebble and watched it bounce. "Maybe I should go."

"No, don't go," she said quickly. "It's...it's good to see you."

"It's good to see you too. It's been too long." Wanting to make things right between them and find a common ground so they could forge some kind of friendship while he was home—hell it was well past time he got to know his niece— he held his arms out.

She looked at his outstretched arms, and after a moment of hesitation, she leaned in to him. He went to give her a kiss on the cheek, but she turned, and their lips touched. They both stilled, and she sucked in a breath.

"Sorry. I..." he began, barely able to keep a coherent thought as the sweetness of her mouth, the softness of her lips took him right back to the day they'd made love.

"Chalk!" Ava squealed, breaking the tension between them.

"How nice." Rachel clapped her hands and stepped back from him.

Kyle shook his head to clear it, and tried for casual. "I

hope it's okay. I had no idea what to get a four-year-old girl. My buddy, Cole, has a daughter Ava's age and suggested chalk." He grinned and nudged Rachel with his shoulder. "Good thing too, I probably would have bought her a train."

Rachel laughed. "Chalk is perfect. She loves to draw. As you can tell she's kind of a girly girl and wouldn't know what to do with a train."

"Like her mom," Kyle said.

She put her hands on her hips and seemed to take offense. "I wasn't a girly girl."

"Sure you were." He rolled a shoulder. "But there's nothing wrong with that, as long as you have the skills to hold your own. You never had to worry about that though." He nudged her playfully. "James and I always had your back."

At the mention of James they both seemed to stop breathing, their eyes locking.

"Mommy, can I draw?" Ava said.

"Sure." Rachel sounded breathless as she turned away from him to ruffle Ava's hair. "Let's head home and you can draw on the driveway." She grabbed Ava's hand and started for the gate. Kyle hung back, his gut tightening as they walked away. He was about to head back to his motorcycle, to go numb himself with a few beers at Sky Bar, when Rachel cast a glance over her shoulder. "Aren't you coming?" she asked.

"I wasn't... I didn't..."

She checked her watch then arched a brow. "Have you had lunch?"

"No."

"Then come on. I'll make you something to eat." Her gaze moved down his body, a leisurely stroll that had his muscles tightening. Jesus, when she looked at him like that, it was all he could do not to drag her back into his arms and give her a proper kiss. "You look like you've been living off rations for too long."

He laughed, the tension easing between them. "And I don't think I'll be stopping anytime soon. I've tasted your cooking, remember?" he teased.

She put her hand on her hip and feigned offense. "I've come a long way since I burnt those grilled cheese sandwiches, you know."

He caught up to them and slowed his pace as they walked the short distance to her small house. Ava chatted on endlessly as she skipped along. He shot a glance around the neighborhood. It was a nice place, filled with kids and families, but it was a far cry from the house she and James had moved into after getting married—a wedding gift from his parents. Even though the newlyweds had just been starting out, living in the wrong part of town with a baby on the way was out of the question for his folks.

"How long have you been home?" They moved down the sidewalk, Ava singing some song at the top of her lungs.

"This morning."

"You just got in?"

Her arm brushed his and he tried not to react, but being close to her was messing with his mind. "Yeah."

She looked a little hesitant when she asked, "Have you seen your parents yet?"

He inched away and put his hands into his pockets. "No."

She nodded and went quiet, staring at her flip-flops as she walked. "Where are you staying?"

"My buddy, Jack, has a room above his motorcycle shop."

She gave a slow shake of her head. "Your parents aren't going to like that."

"You know we don't exactly get along."

"I know," she said, her voice soft.

Of course she knew, because she didn't get along with

them either. James might not have been able to see it, but his folks weren't very nice to Rachel. They were too worried about appearances and couldn't see beyond what they deemed her lower class stature. He fisted his hands inside his pockets, hating how judgmental they were. Rachel was sweet, kind, the nicest girl he knew. Now that James was gone, did she have any kind of relationship with his parents?

He looked at Ava climbing the stairs to the front door, the back bow on her little pink princess dress flopping behind her. He wasn't sure how to bring it up, so he bluntly asked, "Do they see Ava?"

She smiled and started up the stairs behind her daughter. "They do, and they spoil her like crazy."

Kyle grabbed the rail, which wobbled in his hand as he took the stairs two at a time. "Good."

She fished her key from her pocket and tried to open the door. She leaned into it, giving it a good hard shove with her shoulder. "It sticks."

The door banged open and hit the wall with a thud. Kyle followed her in and looked at the hole in the wall where the knob had smashed through numerous times. "You need to get this fixed." He examined the door, checking the seal and hinges.

"I just...I haven't had a chance to call anyone in. I'm not home in the day, and nights I'm busy with Ava."

Ava skipped down the hall. "Mommy, can we have chicken nuggets?"

"No. We're having turkey wraps and veggies, remember?"

Kyle followed her into the kitchen and glanced around. Her home was warm and cozy, toys strewn about and things out of order, so different from the home he'd grown up in. It reminded him of her first apartment, and he liked it. He liked it a lot.

"Ava, can you please grab the wraps from the fridge."

Rachel opened the cupboard, held up by one squeaky hinge, and removed three plates and three water glasses.

Ava pulled the fridge open and gripped a plate with tiny hands. She wobbled a little as she carried it to the table.

"Whoa. Here, let me help." Kyle reached for the plate.

She twisted so he couldn't help. "I can do it," she said lifting her chin as she awkwardly set it down.

Kyle bit back a grin and held his hands up, palms out. "Sorry."

Rachel laughed. "She might be Princess Ava, but she's very independent."

"I can see that."

She gestured toward the fridge. "Can you grab the juice?"

"Sure." Kyle opened the fridge and pulled out the container of apple juice. He filled the three glasses and leaned around Rachel to put the empty jug on the counter near the sink. She turned, and all of a sudden her mouth was right there, inches from his. Heat flooded him, and he breathed in the sweet scent of her skin, the floral fragrance of her shampoo. Raspberries. She always smelled like fresh-picked raspberries. His cock thickened, his heart hammered and it was all he could do not to help himself to another taste of her.

"Oh, sorry." She ducked under his arm.

She moved around him and under the guise of securing the container on the counter, he stood with his back to her and took a moment to compose himself. Christ, when it came to her he was weak—a fucking greedy bastard. Common sense dictated he leave, run in the opposite direction and stay as far away from her as possible. He'd taken advantage of her once, and no way in hell was he going to do it again. But Ava was his niece, and James would have wanted him to get to know her, so he had to get his shit together and be the man they all needed him to be.

After gaining a modicum of control, he turned, folded his

arms across his chest and leaned against the counter. With her back to him, Rachel divvied up the sandwiches and filled each plate with carrots, celery and a small bowl of dip.

Ava stood by the garden door off the kitchen, twisting the lock. "Mommy, can we eat at the picnic table?"

Rachel shot her daughter a look, then glanced at Kyle. "I'm not sure Uncle Kyle can fit."

Was she serious? He smoothed his hand over his stomach. He might have missed a few workouts while traveling, but he wasn't in that bad of shape. "Make up your mind, Rach. Earlier you said I looked like I was living off rations, and now you're saying I'm too big for a picnic table. I'm pretty sure I can fit."

Rachel laughed with him. "Okay, let's go see then." She balanced her plate, picked up her juice and opened the back door. The hinges moaned like a wounded animal. The place was homey but it was missing a man around the place, someone to help with all the repairs. He'd only been in the hall and kitchen and so far there were a lot of them.

Ava rushed out ahead of them, carrying her plate and drink. "Slow down, Ava," Rachel warned as she hurried down the stairs leading to the small backyard.

Kyle followed them out, and laughed when he saw Ava take a seat at the small, pink and white children's picnic table. Son of a bitch. So this is what she meant. Rachel was grinning at him but he was determined to fit. He went down the stairs ahead of her, put his plate on the table, and scratched the back of his head. He had no idea how he was going to get his legs into that small opening, only that he was damn well going to do it.

"We can sit here." Rachel pointed toward the two lawn chairs.

"Nope, if Ava wants to eat at the picnic table, I'm going to eat at the picnic table."

"As stubborn as ever, I see."

He put one leg through and contorted his body. Stubborn or stupid. It was a fine line.

Ava squealed, her eyes wide. "Uncle Kyle," she said, her drink nearly spilling as the table slid on the grass. "You're too big!"

"No I'm not. Look." With one leg through the hole he straddled the bench seat and bit into his sandwich like it was the most comfortable position in the world. It wasn't.

Rachel dropped down next to Ava. The smile on her pretty face as she rolled her eyes at him was worth the pain. It was good to see her happy. They all dug into their food and he looked around the yard. She had a small shed, and a few toys were scattered throughout. His gaze followed the clothesline from the house to a thick tree trunk, but that towering oak screamed for a tree house. He'd always wanted one growing up, but his mother said it was too much of an eye sore and didn't fit in with their professionally designed garden.

Off in the distance a dog barked, and Ava pouted. "Mommy..." she whined, but Rachel shook her finger.

"Ava, you know it's not fair to a dog to be locked in the house all day while I'm at work."

Ava dipped her carrot into the dressing, took a big bite and said, "But I can take him to Miss Tammy's when I go."

Rachel looked at Kyle. "Miss Tammy is her sitter." She turned back to Ava. "Miss Tammy is not able to take care of a dog while she's taking care of all the children she watches."

He could almost hear the wheels in the girl's head spinning. "Lindsay has a daddy, and she doesn't have to go to a daycare. If I had a daddy, then you could stay home like Lindsay's mom and we could get a puppy."

Rachel dropped the carrot stick she was about to take a bite of. She looked down at her plate, hurt and sadness registering in her eyes. "Ava," she began, her voice a bit shaky.

"How about this," Kyle piped in. "My good friend, Gemma, runs a dog shelter. I'll take you there to play with the dogs any time you want." Ava squealed and he said, "I'll even do one better. Some of the guys train those dogs out at the old compound. I can take you with me." He looked at Rachel, who was staring at him like he'd grown a second head. "If your mom says it's okay, of course."

"Mommy, can I? Can I? Please, please, can I?"

"You...you would do that?" Her brow furrowed, her lashes blinking rapidly.

"Absolutely. I want to spend some time with her anyway. This is perfect."

"Is it safe? I mean are the dogs friendly?"

Protectiveness moved through him, for mother and daughter. He picked up his juice and took a swig, swallowing down the bevy of emotions he had no idea how to handle. "I wouldn't take her if they weren't, Rach. I'd never put Ava in any kind of danger. You know that, don't you?"

"Yeah, I do," she said quietly. They exchanged a long look, then she flicked Ava a glance. "I guess it's okay, then."

Ava jumped from the table, went down on her hands and knees and pretending she was a dog started barking. Rachel shook her head.

"Are you sure about this? She has a *lot* of energy."

He put his glass back down on the plastic table. "I'm sure."

"Okay. Ava sit back down and finish your lunch, then you can use your chalk."

She climbed back in beside her mother and started talking endlessly about the dogs as they finished eating. They cleaned their plates, took the dishes inside and stepped back out front so Ava could use her chalk on the driveway.

Kyle took a seat on the steps and Rachel sank down beside him as Ava sat on the pavement and tore into her box of chalk. Kyle smiled as he watched her. Rachel was doing a great job with her daughter. It couldn't be easy to single handedly raise a child while working full time. Honestly, she didn't have to work, not with the insurance money she received after losing James. But Rachel had always been independent, and had always worked for everything she owned. Perhaps she needed to prove she could stand on her own two feet because his mother thought she was a gold digger. Rachel prided herself on her independence and was worthy on her own merits.

"This is a nice neighborhood," he said.

"Your parents weren't all that happy with me moving out of the house they bought us. But after...well, it was just too big for the two of us." She gave a sad laugh. "That's not entirely true. I never liked it anyway, and wanted to be somewhere where there were kids around for Ava."

Kyle looked up and down the street. The houses were close together, lots of kids playing in their yards, and the neighborhood playground and pool was within walking distance. This community had Rachel written all over it but James would have wanted the big mansion and the fancy cars to keep up appearances—and keep his mother happy. Rachel would have hated all of that.

His next thought hit like a grenade. She'd loved his brother, of that he had no doubt, but had she been happy? As he chewed on that, they both went quiet, lost in their own thoughts.

Her leg bumped his, and he angled his head to see her. She watched her daughter with love in her eyes, but those big brown eyes also held the strain of shouldering so much responsibility. She was strong and independent, yes, but the loss of a loved one had been hard on her in so many ways.

The need to help out while he was home pulled at him. He wasn't about to take over where his brother had left off, but James would have wanted him to help her. He was sure of it. Would she accept his assistance if he offered it? Or would having him around remind her too much of her loss?

"What?" she asked, as he gazed at her.

He shook his head. He'd been so lost in thought he hadn't realized she was staring back. "Nothing."

She was about to press when her phone rang. "I'll be right back." She jumped up, then hesitated. "Can you keep an eye on Ava for me?"

"Sure."

Rachel disappeared inside and he pushed off the steps to look over the flowers and rainbows Ava was drawing. He grinned. Oh yeah, she was a real girly girl, like her mother. But with no father in the picture, no one needed a man's influence more than her. While he was in town, he planned to give it to her.

He dropped down beside her. "Have you ever played hopscotch?"

She crinkled her nose, a familiar habit of her mother's.

"Nope," she said.

"Want me to teach you?"

"Okay."

He pointed to the sidewalk. "You go find us two small rocks, but don't go on the road."

Kyle grabbed the chalk and drew the hopscotch grid. Ava came back with two rocks, and Kyle positioned her in front of the first box. He went down on one knee and started to explain the game, but Rachel came from the house, her brow furrowed, her mouth turned down in a frown.

Unease tightened his gut and he stood. "What's wrong?"

"The sitter called. Her two kids have chicken pox. I have to find a replacement before Monday." She tapped her phone on her chin, and looked down in thought. "I don't really have anyone." Her hair fell over her back when she lifted her head and met his glance. She pinched her lips together, then said, "I suppose I could ask your mother. It would only be for a few days."

"I'll do it."

"What? No. You just got back and don't need—"

"I want to." This would be the perfect opportunity to fix some things around her house and give Ava some lessons on life. Back in the day, Rachel had the two Nelson brothers to take care of her, but with no man around the house, Ava would need to learn to stand up for herself, and kick some bully's ass if need be. He looked at Ava. "What do you say, Ava? How about we get you in a pair of coveralls and build a tree house out back?"

Her eyes went saucer wide and she clapped. "Mommy, can I have a tree house?"

"A tree house?"

"Every kid should have a tree house. And you have the perfect tree for it."

Rachel angled her head and narrowed her eyes. "Is this tree house for Ava or for you?"

He grinned. She knew him too well. "Maybe a little bit of both."

"I don't know, Kyle. Tree houses can be dangerous."

"Mommy, please..."

"I can make it low and safe." She continued to hesitate so he tried to seal the deal with, "Maybe that will take her mind off getting a puppy?"

Rachel shook her head, and eyed him. "I'm going to regret this, aren't I?"

"Probably."

**3**

Rachel removed the toothpick from her sandwich, adjusted her chair under the outdoor umbrella, and exhaled an exaggerated breath. Thank God it was lunchtime. Noon couldn't have come quick enough for her. She'd been jittery all morning at work, dropping her scaling tool more than once during a routine cleaning. In fact, she'd been a little off her game since falling on her backside at the park.

The last person she expected to find watching her and Ava was Kyle. *Kyle*. A man she'd loved for so many years now. She'd seen so little of him after the wedding. Then again, he'd made himself scarce even before. But once she married his brother she had no doubt he'd been going out of his way to avoid her after the intimacies they shared at the bluff.

It was clear he carried the guilt of what they'd done like a weighted down rucksack. He'd never want to do anything to hurt his brother. She could relate. She'd never do anything to hurt James—or Kyle—either. In a moment of weakness, she'd given over to the things she felt for him. She never would have allowed that to happen had she still been wearing

James's ring, and while it might have been too soon for them to come together, she comforted herself with the knowledge that she'd been broken up with James at the time, and had no plans to go back.

And now here he was, temporarily home from overseas and taking care of Ava while she was at work. She never should have agreed to it. Having him around and pretending things were normal was too hard on her head and her heart.

Kyle had insisted they put the incident at the bluff behind them, that it was a huge mistake and never should have happened. But putting the night she slept with Kyle behind her was out of the question, because that was the night she'd gotten pregnant with his child. Sweet Ava Marie Nelson was his little girl. She had no idea until years later that the baby was his. James had died of a rare heart disorder, and Ava had to undergo a series of tests to determine if she'd inherited the condition. Rachel had learned two things that day. Her daughter's heart was healthy and strong and her blood type didn't match hers or James's.

Rachel's stomach twisted, and she dropped the sandwich she was about to bite into, her appetite long gone. How could she possibly tell Kyle? He'd hate her for keeping such a huge secret from him, and hate himself even more for betraying his brother on a whole other level.

Still, a man deserved to know he was a father, right?

"You okay?" Sara dropped her tray onto the small café table. The metal chair scraped on the pavement as her best friend pulled it out and plunked herself into it. "You're staring at that cup of coffee like it's your long lost friend."

She forced a smile and met Sara's concerned eyes. Sara, now a doctor who worked two doors down from Rachel, had been her closest friend since high school, and the one who'd taken her under her wing when she'd moved to Austin all those years ago. She was also the one who'd introduced her to the Nelson brothers, stood for her at her wedding and knew her better than almost anyone else. Keeping anything from her was next to impossible. The two things she didn't know, however, the two things no one knew, was who Ava's biological father really was, and how much she loved the man.

"I'm okay," Rachel said.

"Who you trying to convince of that? Me or you?"

Did her friend always have to be so astute? Since there was no point in lying, she said, "Me."

"Okay, spill." Sara popped a potato chip into her mouth.

Rachel pushed her coffee cup away. "It's Kyle. He's back."

"Oh. That was the last thing I expected you to say. I was talking to Caleb last night and he didn't mention anything."

"I don't think he's been by to see any of the guys yet."

"And yet he came to see you."

"He was anxious to see Ava."

Sara quirked a brow, giving her a look that suggested Ava wasn't the only one he was anxious to see. "How is he?"

"He's good." She forced a laugh, trying to make light of what she was about to say, but it came out sounding more like a strangled cry. "He's actually taking care of Ava this week."

"Really? That's nice. So why do you seem so sad?"

"I'm not. I guess seeing him again..." She let her voice fall off. What the heck was she supposed to say? Seeing him again reminded her how much she loved him? How she was holding a secret that would destroy him?

Sara's voice was soft when she said, "I know. I totally understand."

Rachel nodded. No doubt Sara would have come to the most logical conclusion—Kyle's presence upset her because he reminded her of James. No one needed to know the real reason.

Sara went quiet for a long time, then she reached out and

touched Rachel's hand. "You love him." It was a statement, not a question.

Rachel's head jerked back with a start. "What? Of course I don't," she countered, the denial spilling from her lips.

"Rachel, it's me." Sara glanced around, then lowered her voice. "I know you love him. You've always loved him."

Wait! Maybe Rachel was simply reading more in to this. Maybe Sara was simply stating that she loved him, not that she was *in* love with him. "Yes, of course I love him," she responded, playing it off. "He *is* James's brother."

Sara let her hand go and reached for her soda. "You know that's not what I mean."

Her nerves twisted. "What exactly do you mean?"

"I've seen you around him, the way you look at him, touch him. You love him. Just like you loved James."

She shook her head. "I married James. I loved him."

"I know you did, but that doesn't mean you weren't in love with Kyle too. You can love two people equally, you know."

Rachel sat there, guilt eating at her as her heart crashed against her chest. She never wanted to hurt James, but it was true, she did love Kyle, as much today as always. She took a big breath and let it out slowly.

"Sara, it's not—" she looked into her friend's perceptive eyes and her protest died on her tongue. The fight went out of her, the strength to deny her feeling fading like an old black and white photograph. "How long have you known?"

"Since the day I introduced you to the two of them."

A car sped by on the street, its horn blaring at another driver, and she watched it until it disappeared. "How is it possible to love two people at the same time? Is there something wrong with me?"

Sara made a face that suggested she was being ridiculous. "Of course not."

Her gaze dropped to her plate, and she reached for her napkin, twisting it in her fingers. "But it's not normal."

Her friend bit in to her sandwich, chewed, and then, going into professional mode, said, "Actually it is. Empirical evidence proves that someone can love two people at the same time."

The waitress came by, and Rachel asked for a glass of water, needing something to wash away the grit in her throat.

"Rachel, honey..." Sara paused and looked down, like she was choosing her next words cautiously. "James has been gone for two years, and it's time you moved on. You deserve happiness. Everyone does."

Loneliness nipped at her soul. Even if she moved on, went after what her heart wanted, then what? She'd endured so much loss over the last decade—her father's death, James, and then her mother. She couldn't give herself over to her feelings for Kyle only for him to up and leave again. It would surely kill her.

"Sara—"

"Ask yourself this. Why haven't you been able to move on?"

*Kyle...*

"All I'm saying is this. Take what you need, give what you can, and forgive the rest."

"That's pretty profound. Even for you."

Sara nodded, and popped another potato chip into her mouth. "My yoga teacher said that once." A beat passed and she continued with. "Go for it, Rachel. Go after what you want. Don't you think that's what James would want? For you to find love again and be happy?"

The waitress came back with her water, and she took a much needed pull from the straw. She pushed the glass away, planted her elbows on the table and rested her chin in her palms. She let loose a long sigh. "I don't think I want to talk about this anymore."

"Okay, but I think you should take this time to see if there could be more between you two."

"Even if I did, he's leaving after Easter."

"That's a couple weeks away."

"Are you suggesting an affair?"

"I'm suggesting you give him a reason to stay."

Damned if she didn't have one hell of a reason. Kyle was a man of character. If she told him about Ava, he'd stay and do the right thing. He'd hate her, and himself, of that she was certain, but he'd stay for his daughter. She'd never want him to feel trapped, and if he stayed she wanted to be a part of the reason too.

Rachel turned her head and twisted her ponytail, a heaviness falling over her. "It's complicated."

"Then *un*complicate it. Life is short."

*Don't I know it.*

Rachel glanced at her watch and called the waitress over to pack up her untouched sandwich. She'd be starving by her afternoon break and might be able to eat it then. "I need to get back."

"Okay, but just think about what I said. It's time for you to move on and go after what you want."

Rachel's head was swimming as she made her way back to work. She lost herself in the monotony of her job, and the rest of the day zipped by in a blur, her thoughts on Kyle, and Ava, the tree house they were building. By the time five o'clock came around, she hopped into her car and drove home. She pulled into her driveway, parking behind the truck Kyle had borrowed from Jack and showed up in earlier this morning. The sound of a hammer hitting nails reached her ears as she exited her car.

She walked around her small house, and when she reached

her back yard, she stopped dead in her tracks, her heart wobbling at the sight of father and daughter. She took in the stack of wood near the tree, and a shirtless Kyle, his skin tanned and slick from the hot desert sun as he showed Ava how to pound a nail into wood.

She'd been lying when she said he looked like he'd been living off rations. He was all broad shoulders and hard muscles. Even though he was big and strong he moved in a graceful, sexy way. Heat flooded her core, making her hyper-aware of how much she wanted to touch him, to run her fingers over each rippling muscle and lose herself in him again.

His hammer stopped midair, and Kyle looked up and gave her a grin that set off a chain of events inside her. She worked to recover, to present normal, even though her knees were trembling so hard she was sure she was going to land on her ass again.

*Take what you want, give what you can, forgive the rest.*

Sara's words pinged inside her head, but she forced them out. Yes, she loved him and needed to move on, but after everything that had happened, everything she was hiding from him, trying to forge a deeper relationship was wrong. Right?

"Mommy," Ava squealed. Dressed in a pair of jean coveralls, a small tool belt around her waist, and her hair in lopsided braids, she came bouncing over. Rachel picked her up and gave her a hug. "Mommy, we had so much fun. Uncle Kyle took me to see the dogs, and then we got some new clothes and boots." She thrust her leg out. "They have a wheel in them so I can kick anything and it doesn't hurt."

"A wheel? Do you mean they're steel-toed boots?"

"Yeah, that's it." Without missing a beat she continued with, "And then we went and got all this wood for the tree house and then he showed me how to use a hammer so I can help."

"Well, aren't you a lucky lady." She glanced up as Kyle came toward them. His thick muscles shifted in ways that had her pulse leaping as he pulled on his shirt and winced as he stretched out one shoulder. Had he hurt it? "I hope she wasn't too much trouble," Rachel said.

He tugged on one of her pigtails. "We had a great day. Didn't we, squirt?"

Ava giggled. "Uncle Kyle calls me squirt."

God, hearing her call him uncle was like a knife to the gut. She needed to tell him the truth. But how?

"Does he now?" Rachel lowered her daughter, her gaze racing over all the supplies. "Looks like you two have your work cut out for you."

Kyle opened his mouth to speak but Ava put her hands on her hips so he stopped to let her have the floor. "It's a hell of a lot of work but it's going to be worth it. Isn't that right, Uncle Kyle?"

Rachel's jaw dropped and Kyle cursed under his breath. He twisted away so she couldn't see him, but it wasn't hard to tell he was holding back a laugh.

"Ava—" Rachel scolded, but Kyle dropped to his knees and put his hands on Ava's shoulders. She beamed up at him, and Rachel's heart nearly split in two.

"That's right, Ava, it's going to be a lot of work but remember what I told you. We don't repeat what we hear at the lumber yard."

She crinkled her nose, cupped Kyle's face and squeezed. "Right, I forgot."

He turned Ava toward the lumber. "Why don't you go put the hammers in the shed?"

"Okay." Ava skipped away, her pigtails flopping over her shoulders.

Rachel put her hands on her hips mimicking Ava as she glared at Kyle. "I think that might be Ava's last trip to the lumber yard."

Kyle climbed to his feet, his look so sheepish all she could do was laugh. "Sorry I guess kids her age are pretty impressionable."

"To say the least."

"I have a lot to learn. I don't know much about kids." He scratched his head. "Are all little girls as chatty as her?"

She laughed and turned to her daughter, who looked absolutely adorable in a work belt, and her new steel-toed boots.

"Thank you for this," she said quietly.

He stepped closer, too close, and her breath caught in her throat. "Thank you," he said, his voice too soft, too low.

"What are you thanking me for? You're the one doing me a favor."

"No, Rach. It's the other way around. Ava is an amazing little girl, and I'm happy that you're letting me be a part of her life." His hand touched her face, the rough calluses on his palm rasping over her skin.

"Why wouldn't I?"

He opened his mouth and closed it again. His shoulders sagged under the weight of his guilt. Did he think she'd keep Ava away because of what they'd done? Heck, he wasn't the only one on the bluff that day. She was about to tell him that when he spoke.

"I should probably get going. I haven't even been by to see my parents."

"I was going to order a pizza," she said quickly. What the hell was the matter with her? She should just let him go before she did something stupid, like take Sara's advice, but she was so afraid he'd leave and never come back again. "Do you want to have a slice with us first?"

"I don't think—"

"Pizza," Ava called out. "Can I have soda too?" Ava came skipping back over.

"Sure." Rachel inched away from Kyle. "You deserve a treat after being so good today. Now why don't you go on in and get washed up."

Ava shaded the late day sun from her eyes and blinked up at her. "Can we eat at the picnic table again?"

Kyle groaned, and Ava giggled.

"How about we eat inside tonight," Rachel said.

Ava grabbed Kyle's hand, giving him no choice in the matter. "Come on, Uncle Kyle. We have to wash up. Mommy doesn't like dirty hands."

Rachel breathed against the tug in the center of her chest as the two people she loved most climbed the steps and entered the house through the kitchen. She followed and worked to get her emotions under control.

She opened the screen door and stilled. It wasn't squeaking. Why wasn't it squeaking? "Did you fix the door?" she called out.

Kyle stuck his head out of the small powder room. "Yeah, it just needed a bit of oil."

She opened and closed it again. Nice. "Thanks." He disappeared back inside the bathroom and the water turned on. They washed up, and Ava chatted on endlessly to him as Rachel grabbed the phone and called her favorite pizza place.

The two came out of the room as she was hanging up, and Rachel opened her cupboard, careful not to pull it from the hinge. It opened with ease. "Kyle—"

"I put some liquid wood filler in this hole, to give the screws something to grab on to." He leaned over her, his breath hot and distracting on her neck as he tested the filler with the tip of his fingers. Her entire body tensed, his closeness messing with her mind as she pictured him touching her body in much the same manner. One spot in particular.

"You...you've been busy," she managed to get out past a tongue gone thick.

"I'm hoping to fix the front door and the hole in the wall soon." He stepped back and she grabbed three drink glasses. "I have to pick up some plaster. We didn't have time for it today."

"You're a man of many talents." She turned and the glasses nearly fell from her hand when she saw the way he was looking at her, or rather her mouth. She remembered what happened the last time he gazed at her like that.

"I want to help out while I'm here, Rach. Just let me know what you'd like fixed and I'll fix it."

She swallowed. "You're on vacation. You don't have to do all this."

"I want to."

"Okay," was all she said, knowing better than to argue. When Kyle set his mind to something, there was usually no swaying him.

"Mommy, can we play Go Fish until the pizza comes?"

Thankful for the distraction, she pointed to the stairs. "Sure. Go grab the cards."

"You remember how to play Go Fish, don't you?" she asked Kyle as she grabbed the bottle of soda from the fridge and filled three glasses, putting a little less in Ava's.

"World champion three years in a row," he said, and Rachel laughed. Ava came back with last year's Easter basket. She plunked it on the table and pulled out the deck of cards.

"The Easter Bunny is coming soon," she said matter-of-factly as she shook the cards from the box. Ava continued to talk about all the chocolate and the things she wanted for Easter as they played. Eventually the pizza came and she packed her cards away.

Thirty minutes later, Rachel closed the lid on the cardboard box, her heart catching as Kyle and Ava played thumb war. Ava squealed with delight as she pinned Kyle's thumb. The normalcy of it all reminded her how much she wanted this, how her little girl deserved a father in her life. Maybe Sara was on to something. Maybe Rachel should see if things could work out between them.

Kyle turned to her and his gaze narrowed. She shook her head to clear it and pasted on a smile. He pushed from the table. "I should probably get going." He rolled one shoulder, and winced when he stretched his arm out.

Ava mimicked him, and Rachel bit back a grin as her heart twisted. "You look like you pulled something. Maybe the tree house can wait."

"This isn't from the tree house. It's from the cot at Jack's place."

Rachel wiped her mouth with her napkin, then reached for Kyle's plate. She stacked it on hers. "Perhaps it's time to consider staying at your parents' place."

He turned his head so Ava couldn't see him and mouthed the words, "No thanks."

Ava finished off her soda and wiped her mouth with the back of her hand. "Mommy, why can't Uncle Kyle stay here?"

Oh, because she was in love with him, and having him under the same roof was too tempting...too dangerous. And of course there was always the fact that she shouldn't be sleeping with a man she was keeping a huge secret from. And getting close to him, and him leaving like he did last time was a risk to both her and Ava's hearts. But of course she couldn't say any of that in front of her daughter.

"Because, uh..."

"He can sleep in one of my bunk beds."

He winked at Ava. "You don't want me in your room, Ava. I snore so loud I shake the walls."

Ava giggled. "No, silly. We can put the bed in the empty room."

*Oh, Ava, you are always so helpful.*

Her glance met and locked with Kyle's, everything about him playing havoc with her body and heart. What if she came out of her room in the middle of the night and found him exiting the bathroom in his boxers? Would she be able to keep her hands to herself? How would he react if she touched him? Touch her in return, or run the other way?

*Find an excuse, Rachel. Find an excuse.*

"The bed is comfortable and it would save you traveling time every morning and night."

*Well done.*

"Are you sure?" he questioned in a soft voice.

She shrugged. "It makes sense."

Ava jumped up and started hopping around like a bunny. "Yay. Uncle Kyle is sleeping over."

*Yay. Uncle Kyle is sleeping over.*

**4**

Like hell it made sense. He was clearly some kind of masochist, a total glutton for punishment. Standing on the front line weaponless would be far easier than sleeping under the same roof as Rachel and not being able to take her into his arms.

Darkness fell over the city as he drove Jack's truck through town, the key Rachel had given him after setting up the bed in the spare room burning a hole in his pocket. He took his time driving to his folks' place, wanting to stay out late and return after Rachel and Ava had gone to bed. He followed the winding road leading to his parents' house and pulled into the long, circular driveway. He parked and sat for a moment before he killed the ignition. He glanced at himself in the rearview mirror, scrubbed his hand over the whiskers on his jaw, and took in the dark circles under his eyes. The last time he'd been to the house was two years ago for his brother's funeral. His mom had begged him to stay home at the time, but he couldn't.

He climbed from the driver's seat, made his way up the walkway and knocked. This was his home, and he didn't need to knock. Hell, he still had a key, but he always felt a little bit like an outsider. The door swung open and when his mother looked at him, tears filled her eyes.

"Hey, Mom."

"Kyle," she cried, and pulled him inside.

He wrapped his arms around her and gave her a hug. He went to pull away but she held him tighter and his heart squeezed. She'd lost one son, and him being overseas was hard on her. He wished he could make it easier on her, but returning home right now was out of the question.

"Who is it?" he heard his father ask from the den.

"Reg…" his mother said though the tears. "It's…"

"It's me, Dad," Kyle called out.

His father came into the room, a huge smile on his face as he held his hand out. Kyle shook it, then his mother ushered him in to the sitting room. He dropped down onto the leather sofa, and his mother hovered over him as his father went to the bar to pour them both a drink.

"When did you get in? How long are you home? Look at you. You're in need of a shave and a good night's sleep. How about some tea? I can make us a pot."

"No, I'm good, Mom. You don't need to wait on me." He leaned forward and braced his arms on his knees. He darted a glance around the room. Nothing much had changed in the two years since he'd been home, except, of course, James was no longer with them. He gestured to her favorite chair. "Have a seat. Relax."

With a big smile on her face, his mother sat, and his father came back and handed him a tumbler with a splash of bourbon in it. He swirled it and took a swig. It burned down his throat.

"I'm home until after Easter," he began, sidestepping her first question.

"That's only two weeks." His mother steepled her fingers,

but behind her smile he could see the worry. She wanted her son home. He couldn't blame her, and someday he'd stay. When the time was right.

"We opened the cottage," she said. "We'll be heading down next week. You'll come, of course." She looked around. "Where are your clothes? Are they still in your truck? Reg, why don't—"

He held his hand up to stop his father. "No, my clothes aren't with me."

His father sat in his recliner, took a swig and zeroed in on him. "Why not, son?"

Kyle braced himself for the lecture "I'm taking care of Ava this week."

The smile fell from his mother's face and her eyes widened. "Ava. What is this all about? Why would you be taking care of Ava? She has a sitter."

He shrugged, brushing it off like it was nothing. "The sitter's kids have chicken pox, so I told Rachel I'd take care of Ava while I was home."

"So you've been to see Rachel already?" Her brow pulled together, her body stiffening. "How long have you been home?"

"Not long. I wanted to see Ava."

His mother crossed her legs, her lips pinched to a thin line. It wasn't his intention to hurt her by not coming to see her first, but every visit ended in a fight. Either with them begging him to stay or telling him he wasn't living up to his potential. As his mother glared at him now, he could already feel a disagreement coming on. He pinched the bridge of his nose to ward off a headache.

His mother lifted her chin. "I could have looked after Ava if she needed a sitter. It's best that you don't spend—"

"It's okay, Mom. I don't mind and it's time I got to know Ava better, don't you think?" His folks exchanged a look.

"What?" he asked, his stomach tightening with unease as something in their look told him they knew how much he loved Rachel.

"You'll be sleeping here though, correct?" his mom asked, her words rushed. "In your old room. It's exactly as it was when you left. I haven't changed a thing."

"No, I'm going to stay at Rachel's place. She has a spare room."

His mother's hand went to her chest, her look appalled. "I don't think that's a good idea."

A muscle in his jaw twitched, and he darted a glance to his father, who was unusually quiet. "Why not?"

His mother lifted her chin. "Think of how it would look, Kyle. What would people say?"

"I don't care how it looks, Mom, and I don't care what people say." He raked an agitated hand through his hair. "I'm staying at her place because it's convenient and easier to take care of Ava."

His mother's nose went a little higher. "Is Ava really the one you're taking care of?"

What the fuck! Anger cut like shrapnel. Christ, he hadn't even been home two minutes and she was starting in on Rachel. "You didn't just say that, did you?"

Her face went poker straight, her shoulders square—a practiced pose. Despite the composed demeanor her voice was elevated when she said, "She tricked one boy into marrying her. I won't let her trick another."

"Tricked?" Kyle jumped to his feet. "She didn't trick James into anything. He loved her, and she loved him. Now Rachel is single handedly raising your granddaughter and doing a hell of a good job. If you feel anything for her it should be respect and admiration."

"Okay, enough." His father put his glass down and stood. He walked over to Kyle, placed his hand on his shoulder and

Kyle prepared for the backlash. Instead, his father said, "It's good to see you, son. Go take care of Ava, and bring her by the house. Maybe we can all get some fishing in at the cottage while you're home, and you know we'd love to have you, Rachel, and Ava join us here for Easter dinner."

Kyle looked at the man who'd been so hard on him over the years, and took in the fine lines bracketing his tired eyes. There was a sadness on his face he hadn't seen before, a real sorrow that tugged on Kyle's heart. The loss of James had been hard on them all.

"I didn't come here to fight." The mellowing of his father had drained the battle from him. But he'd be damned if he was going to let anyone say anything bad about Rachel.

"Why don't we all talk later, after we've all had a good night's sleep?"

Mom stood and smoothed her hand over her hair. "Give Ava a hug for us."

"I will." He followed his father to the front door and was about to leave until his father cleared his throat, the way he always did when things were about to turn serious. Perhaps he hadn't softened after all.

"You don't have to go back, you know."

Kyle gripped the back of his neck, understanding the conversation had shifted from Rachel to the military. "It's my job. It's what I signed on for."

"You know I always wanted you to come work at the firm with me."

He laughed, but it came out sounding strangled. Truthfully, he was happy to watch James take that corner office and fulfill his dreams. But deep inside he felt a little envious, a little left out. James and his dad had grown closer, sharing many inside jokes. Kyle wanted to be a part of it all—to have his own corner office. Heck, he dabbled in the market for fun, and made a load of money. But he'd slacked in school and stayed out of the spotlight.

"Doing what? Sorting mail?"

"You're still young, Kyle. Young enough to go back to school and get a degree."

"I'm not James."

"No you're not, and I'm not asking you to take his place, if that's what you think."

Maybe not. But is that what his mother thought when it came to Rachel and Ava? That he could just step in and take over where James had left off. He would never do that. He turned and opened the door. "I have to run."

"Think about it, okay? And be sure to bring Ava to the lake. We don't see her enough."

He left and hopped in his truck, too keyed up to head back to Rachel's place. Perhaps he'd join the guys at Sky Bar for a drink before he gathered his gear at Jack's and hit the sack. Pulling back into traffic, he headed in the opposite direction. The parking lot was fairly quiet on Monday night, but he was sure he'd find a comrade or two inside to shoot a game of pool with him and take his mind off his trouble for a while.

He walked through the entrance and the second he stepped foot in the dimly lit establishment his mind went back to the night Rachel had come through these doors looking for him. He pushed the events that followed from his mind and zeroed in on Matt and Caleb playing pool. Laughter erupted as Matt sank the eight ball and grabbed the five-dollar bill from the table. Kyle sauntered over.

"Kyle," Caleb said when he saw him.

Matt laid his cue on the table and pulled him in for a hug. "Hey, buddy, when did you get home?"

"Yesterday," he said, and Matt raised his hand to gesture

the waitress to bring another round, then focused back on him.

"How the hell are you, man?"

"Good. Things are good. How about you?"

In typical army doctor fashion, Caleb looked him over. The last time the two had seen each other was at James's funeral. "You're looking good," Caleb said. A beat passed and then, "How are your folks?"

"They're doing well. I was just by to see them." He laughed to make light of the situation. "You know Mom, always trying to get me to move back home."

In a teasing manner, Caleb put his hand on Kyle head and gave a push. "Worried about her baby boy." Then the smile fell from his face. "Have you seen Rachel?"

"Yeah." He nodded. "Actually I'm babysitting Ava while I'm in town."

The two guys exchanged a look. "What?" Christ, did everyone know how he felt about Rachel.

The waitress came with their drinks and he took a huge swig, downing half the bottle in one drink.

"Nothing," they both said.

"She needed a sitter, and from the looks of things, a man around the house."

Caleb eyed him.

"I mean the place is falling apart, and she's so busy she doesn't have time to call anyone in to fix the place. I thought I could help out while I was home." What the hell was he doing? They didn't ask for an explanation, so why did he feel the need to give one. He was acting like he was guilty as hell for something. He turned his attention to the table. "Who wants to play?" He grabbed the rack and pulled the balls from the corners.

"Me." Matt's cell phone pinged and he pulled it from his pocket. "Never mind. Change of plans."

He took in the wide smile on Matt's face. "Your grandma? How is she?"

"She's great actually. But I'm talking about Sky. She moved in to Gran's place with me."

Kyle's head came back with a start. "You and Sky?"

"Yeah. Me and Sky. I'm the luckiest fucking guy in the world."

Caleb laughed and placed his beer bottle on the edge of the pool table. "About fucking time too," he said, like the two were in on some secret. "I couldn't handle any more of his moping."

Matt laughed. "You're channeling Gran." He put his cue away and finished off his beer. He put his hand on Kyle's shoulder. "The wedding is in June. I'd love it if you could come. Bring Rachel."

"I'm leaving at the end of April."

"I'll send the invite anyway." His hand fell away and a seriousness fell over Matt. "It's good to see you, buddy. It's good to have you home."

A lump gathered in his throat. He was tired of running and it did feel good to be home. He missed his time with the guys. He missed his brother, his parents...Rachel. And now with Ava drilling out a special spot in his heart, he was going to miss her too. "Thanks, and congratulations on the engagement. Sky's a great girl. You're a lucky guy."

Matt smiled and went quiet for a moment, like he was remembering something from long ago. "Listen, next weekend we're having a backyard barbeque. A celebration of sorts. Come by. I know everyone would love to catch up."

"Not much to catch up on."

"Garrett, Gemma and their kids will be there. Charlotte is around the same age as Rachel's daughter."

"Ava," he said, his heart warming as he thought about her precociousness.

"So, you'll come? It'll be nice for the kids to get to know one another."

"We'll see. I'll have to check with Rachel." It was true, it would be nice for the kids to get to know each other, and Rachel didn't look like she'd had any kind of adult fun in a long time. Like she'd said, when she wasn't working, she was with her daughter. It might do her good to get out with people her own age. "Wait, what's the celebration for?" he asked.

Caleb put his hand on Matt's shoulder. "Our buddy here passed his MCATs and will be starting med school in the fall."

"You're kidding me?"

"Nope," Matt said. "I got a girl to take care of now." He waved his phone. "And if things go according to plan, me and Sky will be filling Gran's house with kids. So I need to get the hell out of here now. She needs me." He winked. "If you know what I mean."

Matt James. Field ambulance tech turned doctor. He never thought he'd see the day when Matt grew up. Christ, the last he remembered, Matt was still eating peanut butter from the jar. "That's great, Matt. I'm proud of you, buddy."

"What about you?" Matt asked. "Have you thought about what you're going to do when you get out?"

"Not really." If his father had it his way, however, he'd have a nice corner office in Dad's downtown sky rise. Going back to school wasn't out of the question. He'd considered it over the years, but it was always something for later down the road. Unlike Matt, he didn't have to make any *adult* choices. He didn't have a family depending on him, and didn't see that happening anytime soon. While he was sure he'd enjoy invest-ment banking, he and his dad got along about as well as two cats in a duffle bag. Then again, Dad seemed to have mellowed a bit over the years.

"Catch you guys later." Matt turned and hurried toward the back entrance.

Kyle shook his head. "What the hell happened since I've been gone?"

"You mean with everyone getting married and having kids?"

"That's exactly what I mean."

"If you want your mind blown, then let me tell you Luke hooked up with Emery, as in Emery Vincent Taylor, daughter of the man who put him in juvie."

"What the fuck?"

Caleb held his beer up. "I think it's something in the water, which is why when I'm in town, I stick to beer."

Kyle picked up his beer and clinked it against Caleb's. "I hear ya, buddy. You still up in San Antonio?" He walked to the head of the table and broke the balls. They clattered and he sank a low ball.

"Heading back shortly," he explained stealing a glance at his watch. "Had a long weekend and spent it with Matt and Sky. Those two are good together."

When James asked Rachel to marry him and they began down a path that didn't include him, it made Kyle feel like the third wheel. He was glad Sky, Matt and Caleb—all best friends since childhood—found a way to make it work out. Could he have found a way instead of running halfway around the world? Doubtful. Caleb wasn't in love with Sky the way he was in love with Rachel. There was no way he could have stayed and tried to keep things normal.

He took a shot, sank the ball and walked around the table to take another. For the next hour, he hung out with Caleb, the two just shooting the shit until Caleb glanced at his watch again.

"I better hit the road, buddy. Early morning tomorrow." He put his cue away. "I hope to see you at the barbeque."

"Yeah, I might go." Caleb disappeared through the front door and, since it was nearing ten, Kyle could only imagine Rachel and Ava were already tucked in. He couldn't wait to do the same. He was dog-tired. Ava might be a little squirt of a thing, but her energy exhausted him. He jumped in his truck and made his way to Jack's to grab his gear. He snuck in through the back, hoping to avoid a run-in with his friend. The last thing he needed tonight, especially after the argument with his parents, was another interrogation. Jack was a great guy, hell, he loved the man, but he was always sticking his nose where it didn't belong. He'd be the first to question him about Rachel, and the man could smell a lie all the way to Afghanistan.

He grabbed his rucksack and drove back to Rachel's. There was a light on in the upstairs bedroom—her bedroom. Walking quietly, he let himself in, and not wanting to make any noise, he kicked off his boots before making his way up the creaky staircase. He slipped into his room and tossed his bag on the bed. A noise sounded and he stilled, listening for it again. His ears met with silence so he reached into his rucksack and grabbed his shaving kit. He made a quick trip to the bathroom, then noticed Rachel's bedroom light spilling into the hall as he returned to his room.

He pulled off his shirt and, dressed only in his jeans, he threw himself down on his bed and reached for the pillow, only to discover there wasn't one. Shit. Since he wasn't about to bother Rachel, he drove his hand under his head and rested on his forearm. Hell, it wasn't the first time he'd gone without a pillow. He closed his eyes, and despite his exhaustion, sleep wouldn't come. He tossed, flipping to his sides, first right, then left, then on his back again. The bed frame squeaked with each move, even though he'd been trying extra hard to be quiet.

A soft knock sounded on his door, and his heart jumped.

He threw his feet over the side of the bed and padded quietly across the small bedroom. He inched the door open, and when he found Rachel standing there, dressed in a nightshirt, that hovered mid-thigh, he nearly bit off his tongue. Her hair was loose, a tousled mess, like she too had been tossing and turning only moments ago. The warm bedroom look was so sexy on her it triggered a craving unlike anything before.

As his traitorous cock thickened, his mind went down a path it had no right to travel. His fingers itched to touch, and his mouth watered to taste as his body ached to join with her, to lose himself in the heat between her legs. Holy Christ. He drew a breath, desperate to leash his control.

*Get it together, dude.*

"Hey," he said quietly, glancing past her shoulders to see if Ava was in the vicinity. Her bedroom door was shut. She had to be fast asleep.

"I wanted to make sure you were okay." She spoke in whispered words and her dark lashes blinked rapidly as she looked him over, but he wasn't so sure it was concern he spotted in her eyes.

"I'm okay." He struggled to keep his gaze off the plunging neckline of her nightshirt, and the creamy cleavage that was lasering in on every functioning brain cell, and zapping them dead, one by one. Christ, he was going to need those brain cells, otherwise he'd end up taking advantage of her in a time of vulnerability again. He couldn't let that happen.

Her gaze left his face and lingered on his chest. His muscles spasmed under her scrutiny. "Is your shoulder bothering you?" she asked, her voice sensual, quiet.

He shook the buzz from his head. "No, why?"

"You're tossing and turning a lot." She crinkled her nose and gestured with a nod to the wall separating their rooms. "I could hear the bed frame squeaking," she explained. "And I thought you might need something."

Oh, he needed something all right.

"I have some joint and muscle ointment, it helps with pain and swelling."

Uh, not the kind of swelling he had.

She lifted her hand to show him a tube of anti-inflammatory gel. He hadn't noticed it earlier. No, he'd been too busy looking at the curves in her nightshirt, the way her nipples were poking against the thin fabric. Would she be pantyless too?

*Fuck me.*

"This stuff is great," she whispered. "You should try it."

Needing something to do with his hands before he grabbed her by the waist and pulled her in for a kiss, he reached out and took it from her. He held the capped end in one hand and tapped the bottom of the tube against his palm, fighting valiantly to suppress his urges.

"Thanks. I'll give it a try."

"Here, let me help." She reached for the tube with shaky hands, unscrewed the cap and poured a generous amount into her palm. She stepped closer, and her warm, sweet scent curled around him as her hand went to his shoulder. That first touch penetrated his defenses and a rush of sexual energy hit him so hard, his entire body rippled.

"You're so tight," she said, her voice a breathless whisper. "Maybe you should put off building the tree house."

"No I want to do it for Ava." Christ, was that his voice. He sounded like he'd just eaten a bucket of nails.

His skin began to burn wherever she touched but it had nothing to do with the ointment. The room seemed to grow warmer, the walls closing in on him. Maybe if he got outside he could clear his head.

"Always so stubborn," she murmured, her voice keeping him put. She poured another generous dollop into her palm and went back to rubbing it in, each caress fueling the flames inside him. He turned sideways to hide the swelling in his pants, but when her eyes fell to his bulging zipper, he suspected she could see right through him. "Well this should help, at least."

She was speaking, saying something, but between the mad pounding of his heart and the thrumming in his head, he could barely comprehend. He worked to tamp down his desire, but his fucking cock refused to obey.

Her fingers skimmed along his shoulder, then down his arm. He closed his eyes against the flood of heat, unable to breathe past the need clawing at him. Maybe if he took her to his bed—one last time—it would help get her out of his system.

*Shit, get it together, Kyle. You're stronger than this.*

When he opened his eyes again, he found Rachel staring at him, those dark come-hither eyes of hers seducing his last vestige of his control. When it came to her, he was fighting a losing battle.

"Kyle?"

**5**

The intense, almost troubled way he looked at her made her hyperaware of how much she wanted him again. Need raced through her as his eyes moved over her face, her mouth, devouring her like a man driven by more than just desire. There was a sense of urgency in him unlike anything she'd ever felt before. It was both frightening and exhilarating.

"Kyle," she whispered again. His name lingered in the air as she parted her lips, welcoming his kisses, his touches. Even though she had no idea where they stood, or what would happen tomorrow when the lust cleared from their brains, she was powerless to deny her needs or question the logic in them coming together intimately again. Tonight she wanted to feel, not think, and prayed that come tomorrow there were no regrets, for either of them.

His nostrils flared as his hand snaked out and grabbed her nightshirt. He bunched the material into his fist and gave a hard yank. She jerked forward, her body crashing against his. He hissed as they collided, and his lips came down hard. His mouth moved over hers. His kisses were carnal, ravenous, and so damn demanding all she could do was close her eyes and revel in the sensations.

Her body pushed against his, her stomach rubbing against the steel erection straining behind his worn jeans. There was no denying that he wanted this as much as she did, but would he run away in the clarity of morning, like he did last time? Her stomach clenched. Now that he was back in her life, how would she ever survive him leaving?

A growl crawled out of his throat as the air around them charged with enough sexual energy to set off a nuclear plant. Her body trembled, her nipples hardening even more as they poked against her nightshirt and brushed against his bare chest. He deepened the kiss, his tongue slashing against hers. Her heart slammed in her chest. Oh God, she needed…

"Yes," she murmured, and that one word seemed to do something to him. He reached over her shoulder and closed the door, then backed up toward the small bed, dragging her with him.

Her hands slid around his back, exploring his hardness as his body tensed beneath her fingers. She breathed in his familiar scent as her heart twisted with the love she felt for him. Her thoughts fragmented when his hands slipped under her shirt and skimmed along her sides, going higher and higher until he stroked the outer slopes of her breasts. Those work-roughened hands of his kneaded her body, the scraping of his calluses amping her excitement to a whole new level. Kyle was smart, smarter than he let on, but he was also a man who wasn't afraid of manual work or getting his hands dirty.

Something about his ruggedness appealed to the woman in her. But she couldn't think about that any longer, not when the rough pads of his thumbs were coming perilously close to her nipples. She moved back, pulling away from his chest so he could touch her, taste her. Oh, what she'd do to feel the heat of his mouth on her body, between her legs.

She arched into him, letting him know in no uncertain terms what she wanted, needed from him tonight. His fingers found her nipples, his thumbs brushing urgently over them, his touch commanding yet soft. Her breath grew shallow and when their eyes met and locked, they exchanged a long, heated look, one that said no matter what happened tomorrow, tonight was a different story.

Her hands left his body and she peeled her shirt over her head, tossing it onto the unmade bed. Eyes that looked tortured, delirious with need, went to her breasts as she stood before him in nothing but her panties. She hadn't planned for this to happen, and thanked the Lord that she had the foresight to wear her favorite black lace, not her normal comfy cotton that had zero sex appeal.

Then again, maybe on some level she'd hoped this would happen.

Her eyes raked over him in return, her fingers itching to explore his body, to take his hardness in her hands, her mouth. Her body quivered. She'd missed him so much. Missed his smell, his touches, his laugh, his smile. When was the last time he smiled or had any kind of fun? Then again, she could ask herself that same question.

He cupped the back of her neck and pulled her closer. His lips crashed down on hers again, then brushed along her cheek, dusting kisses down her jaw as his hands moved around her back, pulling her impossibly tighter against his body.

His hands slid to her backside and he squeezed her ass, his mouth going to her neck. A shiver moved through her when he found the sensitive spot he'd discovered all those years ago. She writhed against him and he trailed his tongue lower. Her hands moved to his hair, and she raked her fingers through it when his mouth found her breasts.

He made a slow pass with the soft blade of his tongue, and heat exploded through her. "Yes," she murmured holding him against her. He licked again, his tongue warm, lethal against her bare flesh. His teeth clamped around her nipple, and he bit down with enough pressure that she felt it all the way to her core. Her sex quivered, and moistened in anticipation. Her breasts filled with blood and swelled, and she could almost feel the tension rising in him as he licked, nibbled and sucked his fill.

Heat tugged low in her pelvis and her body grew so needy standing became difficult. His hands slid along her inner thighs, and he pushed her panties aside, running his finger along the lacy slip of material. His knuckle nudged her clit, and a gasp caught in her throat. Her hands tightened in his hair, waiting...just waiting for him to touch her. He was toying with her, teasing her to the point of madness. Frustration grew inside her. She needed so much more.

"Please touch me," she begged, her words tumbling out in a whisper as she rocked her hips, to force his finger to the spot that needed him the most.

Kyle stopped touching her and pulled away, leaving cold where there was once heat. Her stomach dropped, a commotion breaking out inside her. Was he having second thoughts? His chest rose and fell erratically, and his eyes latched on hers as his hands went to the button on his pants. He tore at it then released his zipper in a rush. Relief moved through her. He shoved his jeans down his legs and kicked them away. He was moving fast, too fast. She was sure any second now he was going to rip her panties from her hips, toss her on the bed and take her hard and fast. While she liked that idea, she needed to touch him in the worst way.

When he reached for his boxer shorts, she closed her hand over his. "Stop," she pleaded.

His body tightened, and he pinched his eyes shut. A strange, strangled noise caught in his throat. "Jesus," he said, that one word so strained she could barely hear it. The sound of his indrawn breath filled the sudden silence. He began to move away, but she shook her head, and squeezed his hand to still him.

"No, Kyle," she whispered in a haze of arousal. "I want you to slow down. I want to watch you undress. I want to touch you."

His muscles bunched. "Oh, Christ," he said on a growl, his cock straining so hard against his shorts she thought they might rip open.

She stepped up to him and put her hands on his body, running her fingers over the hard planes and contours, and just taking a quick moment to enjoy the feel of him beneath her palms. He was a fighter, a soldier, the toughest guy she knew. But seeing the way he was coming unhinged from her unhurried exploration, fired her up so fast and so hot she feared she might go up in a burst of flames. But it would be worth it because she liked this side of Kyle. Liked the way he let down his guard and reacted to her.

She ran her hands lower, following the dark line of hair leading to his boxers. He trembled when she slipped her fingers inside the thick elastic band and shoved them down his hips until she freed his cock. Her head dipped and she gazed at his erection for a long time, taking pleasure in his girth and length, the pre-come pooling on his crown. She moistened her lips and took him into her hands, enjoying the way he pulsed in her palms as she ran them from crown to base, dipping into his liquid heat to use as lubricant. He cupped the back of her head, his fingers tangling in her hair.

"That feels so good," he murmured and let his head fall back, his eyes closed.

He rocked into her hands, and as his hips powered forward, she pressed her lips to his chest. The saltiness of his skin danced on her tongue as she trailed her mouth lower, and when she sank to her knees, he stilled. The hard tug on her hair forced her eyes to his.

Confusion furrowed his brow as his eyes latched upon hers. With his other hand, he swept her hair from her face and his throat made a noise as he swallowed.

"Rach?" he questioned, so much emotion, tenderness in his voice, she nearly forgot how to breathe. "Baby, what are you doing?"

She had no idea why he was so shocked. Had no woman ever done this for him before? If not, she was going to rectify that, because she wanted to taste him, to savor every inch of his body and give him the same pleasure he was giving her. Instead of answering, she leaned forward and drew him into her mouth, taking him in until his crown hit the back of her throat. A shudder moved through him. He was big, too big. There was no humanly way she could close her mouth around every inch, but she was damn well going to do her best. She loosened her throat, and leaned in to him.

"Oh, fuck." He gripped the sides of her head and he curled his fingers through her hair.

He held her hair back and watched her pleasure him. Wanting to give him a show, to make this good for him, she moaned in pleasure and he swelled even more as she greedily took him more deeply than was comfortable. She massaged his balls until they drew up into his body and ran her tongue over him, lapping at the juices spilling from his crown. While she'd like to stay at his feet all night, until he released in her mouth, from the sounds coming from his throat she guessed it was becoming too much for him—and that he had other plans.

"You're fucking killing me, baby." He groaned. "Come here." He pulled her to her feet, her softness colliding with his hardness as their bodies meshed.

His mouth found hers, his hand racing over her curves as he turned her until the backs of her knees hit the bed. With a little shove she fell backward. He sank to the floor between her legs and grabbed her thighs. He gave a tug and dragged her until her ass was on the edge of the bed. She went up on her elbows to see him, and the desire reflecting in his eyes licked her from head to toe. She was sure she'd never been so turned on in her life.

With eyes the darkest shade of blue she'd ever seen, he tapped the side of her ass, and pleasure resonated through her. "Lift," he growled.

She did as he requested, and he slid her panties down her legs. His breath was so hot on her flesh she was sure she was going to orgasm from the heat alone. Warmth spread through her as he brushed his mouth over her inner thighs. Once he had her completely naked, he spread her legs and placed them over his shoulders. He closed his eyes, and leaned over her, bending her knees toward her sides. He pressed his mouth to her stomach and breathed deeply, like he was savoring the scent of her skin. He slid lower, until his mouth was right there...right where she needed it most.

"You are perfect," he murmured from between her legs. The need in his voice, the intimacy in his tone, curled her toes and fired her senses. His hands slid over her stomach, her hips and outer thighs. As he reacquainted himself with her body, she quivered from the inside out, needing him so badly if he didn't soon touch her she was going to splinter into a million tiny pieces. "So fucking perfect."

Her breath caught when his tongue finally found her sex.

"Kyle," she whispered with effort, a long, slow moan catching in her throat as she collapsed back down on the bed.

Pinned beneath him, he parted her lips with his fingers, and using the rough pad of his thumb he circled her clit. Slow, torturous strokes that drove her mad and took her to the precipice in record time. As soft quakes began in her core, his tongue replaced his finger, the wet heat singeing her sex and shutting down her brain. Sparks shot through her body and she trembled as he nurtured an orgasm from her in the most delicious ways.

His fingers stroked deep, and her muscles rippled as desire flared inside her. She gave a broken gasp as he touched her in places so deep she thought she'd died and gone to heaven. She gripped the bed sheets, ripping the corners from the sides as she arched in to him and concentrated on the erotic sensations.

His tongue centered on her clit and he applied more pressure—the perfect amount of weight to take her where she needed to go. As her blood boiled under his artful manipulation, every nerve ending fired and sizzled through her body. She whimpered and tossed her head from side to side. So. Much. Pleasure.

His tongue stroked her clit as his finger plunged hungrily, long, luxurious strokes that escalated the tension inside her. She closed her eyes against the duel assault, losing herself in him completely. While she never wanted the moment to end, she had no idea how much longer she could hold on. Her hands went to her breasts and she touched her nipples, rolling them between her fingers.

Kyle cursed from between her legs and she glanced down to find him watching her. She grinned and squeezed her nipples harder, loving the way he reacted. Still cursing, he turned his attention back to her sex and buried his face in deeper. His tongue swirled and stroked, his fingers pressed hungrily. The pleasure was exquisite. She whimpered and her body tingled all over. Her breath caught and the world around her faded. The only thing that mattered was this man, and what he was doing to her.

He stroked with expertise, and when she lifted her hips to force him in deeper, a violent shudder overtook her. She gave a breathy moan and let go, her muscles clenching and spasming with the hot flow of release.

"Fuck, yes," he growled as she rippled around his finger, beneath his expert tongue. He lapped at her, drawing out her pleasure until the spasm subsided. Her heart raced and it took effort to breathe.

She needed a moment to recuperate, but he gave her no reprieve. Instead, he grabbed something from his pants, climbed over her body and repositioned her on the bed. His breathing was so labored, so harsh, she could feel his heart crashing against her chest.

She reached out and traced the pattern of his face, tracing the outline of his jaw as he leaned into her. "Kyle," she murmured against his cheek, needing him as much as he needed her.

"I need to be inside you," he said, his voice barely recognizable. He tore into a condom and quickly sheathed himself. In one fluid movement he grabbed her legs and spread them, then fell over her body. He positioned himself at her opening and brushed his tongue along the seam of her lips. "Tell me you want that too."

"I want that too," she whispered, his intensity scaring her a little.

His tongue pushed between the slit of her lips and plundered her mouth, then in one quick thrust he drove into her. The fit was tight and the spreading of her walls tore the air from her lungs. He stilled, like he was waiting for her to catch her breath. She sucked in air, and when she expelled it, he pulled out and rammed back inside again. Her arms slipped around his shoulders, her fingers slicking over his passion-drenched flesh as he rocketed in and out of her, like all his control was going down in a burst of flame. She moved beneath him, and he gave a lusty groan as her sex clenched around his girth.

His mouth moved to her neck and he buried his face in the soft hollow of her throat. She wrapped her legs around him and met and welcomed each thrust, encouraging him to give himself over to the things he was feeling...the things he needed.

He grabbed her shoulders, and was panting heavily, the heat of his mouth fanning over her body. His fingers bit into her flesh, hard enough to leave a bruise. She bit her lip, her heart stuttering with the possessive way he was taking her.

"So good," she murmured, warmth flooding her.

He angled for deeper thrusts and the depth of penetration pushed her desires higher and higher. The crescendo of their union took her to the peak a second time, and she gave herself over to the sensations. A shiver wracked her body. She sucked in air and swallowed against the dryness in her throat.

"Kyle," she murmured, scratching her nails over his back as her cream trickled down her thighs.

Kyle growled, his body tightening all over. He pumped once, twice then threw his head back as he let go. He pulsed inside her, and she closed her eyes, her sex muscles squeezing his cock in response.

Oh. My. God.

Her thoughts whirled, her brain wobbly like the buzz from a fine wine. Kyle collapsed on top of her as she basked in the glow of amazing sex. She ran her hands over his back, his muscles vibrated and danced beneath her touch. His breath was hot on her neck as he struggled to catch it. She touched his hair, felt the dampness. A bone-deep warmth flowed through her.

He shifted his hips and inched out of her. The loss flooded her with a different kind of need. Thick muscles flexed as he turned away and discarded the condom. She touched his back, not wanting to break contact. Her fingers trailed over his damp skin, a melee of emotions pressing against her chest.

He fell in beside her, a new intimacy between them. She rolled on the small mattress toward him and breathed in his scent. Cloaked in sexual contentment, she nestled against his chest and his arm went around her. His heart was strong and powerful as it beat against her cheek. She snuggled closer, and he pulled the blankets up. It felt so good to be held by him. She closed her eyes, and sank into him. Sleep pulled at her, and her eyes slipped shut. Her breathing leveled and she could feel herself drifting, but something unsettling pulled her awake. Something that filled her with dread. She listened to Kyle breathe, took in the stiffness of his body. He was far from relaxed, and he was quiet.

Too quiet.

Too still.

Her stomach dipped, her euphoria disappearing. She knew him well enough to know something was going on inside his head. She scraped her teeth over her kiss-swollen lip and drew a fortifying breath.

"Kyle," she asked in a soft voice, her hand going to his chest.

"Yeah."

"You okay?"

He inched back, rolled to his side, and went up on one elbow. It wasn't just a physical retreat, it was an emotional one. He'd done the same thing with her once before.

"Rach." He brushed her hair from her cheek. His weary

gaze moved over her face, a slow careful assessment. She took in the worry lines bracketing his eyes. "Are you okay?" His voice came out tight.

Her blood turned cold, her throat closing over. "Yes," she managed to get out, even though it was a lie.

"Listen." He exhaled slowly and she braced herself. God, if he left now, disappeared from their lives again, she had no idea how she'd handle it. Her stomach knotted and she steadied herself. He peered at her, his forehead creasing. "What we did. It was..."

"Wonderful," she said.

"Right, wonderful, but we can't let this happen again." A pause and then, "You know that, right?"

She went quiet for a long time, trying to pull herself together as she digested and chewed on his words. If what they were doing was so wrong, then why did it feel so right?

"Yeah," she said quietly, agreeing only because she feared he'd run the other way. She worked to harden herself, to tamp down the things she felt for him.

He cupped the back of her neck, and as his thumb traced her hairline in a tender way, it instantly took her back to the place where emotions ruled. Her heart missed a beat. Blue eyes locked on hers and he rested his forehead against hers, the closeness she felt with him completely overwhelming her.

One arm circled his neck to hold him, but he gripped it, pulled it away and placed it at her side.

"It shouldn't have happened in the first place," he whispered.

In a way, he was right. She never should have allowed it to happen, at least not before she told him the secret she'd been keeping from him. He carried enough guilt as it was. But truthfully, in her heart she knew what they did wasn't wrong. Not when she loved him so much.

He glanced at her apologetically. "I shouldn't have taken... I just...needed..."

She gazed into his stormy eyes and there was something more there, something behind the guilt.

"I needed too," she said, craving the feel of him against her body again.

A strange, surprised look came over his face. He looked at her like he couldn't comprehend the words coming out of her mouth. What? Did he think this was all about him? That because he initiated it, the responsibility for what happened was his? She was a woman with needs too, and she had no trouble owning up to the fact that she wanted him, and this, as much, if not more, than he did. They were both responsible for everything that happened between them.

She was about to tell him all that, even though she suspected he wouldn't believe her, when she heard Ava calling out to her. Since she didn't want her daughter to find her in bed with Kyle, she jumped up and pulled on her nightshirt.

"Rach," he said quietly. "I think I should go."

She struggled to keep her voice level, the tears from spilling. She kept her back to him, and smoothed her hand over her hair. "If that's what you want." She didn't want him to go, it would tear her heart in two, but she wasn't going to keep him here if he didn't want to stay. She'd never want him to feel trapped.

"It's not what I want," he whispered.

She turned to face him, her emotions on a roller coaster ride with no strap to hold them in. "Then what do you want?" she blurted out.

"I...I want us to be friends again."

She nodded, because she wanted that too, but she also wanted more.

"Do you think we could do that?" he asked quietly. "Do

you think we could be friends? You know, hang out like we used to?"

"Yes," she said, even though everything had changed since those carefree days of their youth. There was more going on between them, neither could deny it, but right now maybe they just needed friendship to get them though the next few days—before the secret came out. Her stomach clenched, because once that happened, she feared she wouldn't even have that from him anymore.

$$6$$

The sound of Ava's feet running up and down the hall pulled Kyle awake. With exhaustion pulling at him after a restless night, he stretched his arms over his head and turned toward the window. On the street below he could hear children playing and laughing, and it tugged at something inside him.

All his comrades were getting married and having families. He'd never given it much thought before, because he couldn't imagine a life with anyone but Rachel.

*Rachel.*

Sweet, vulnerable Rachel who he'd once again taken advantage of. He fisted his hair. What the hell had he been thinking? He hadn't been, and that was the problem. One look at her and all his blood went south. He should have stayed strong, never should have taken advantage of her loneliness and dragged her into his bed. What a fucking douche.

A soft knock sounded on his door. "Time to get up, Uncle Kyle."

Kyle smiled and his mood shifted when he heard sweet

little Ava. He was looking forward to hanging out with her today. Facing Rachel after last night? Not so much.

"I'm up," he said. "I'll be right out."

Her feet pounded on the stairs as she ran down the steps, singing some song at the top of her lungs as she chased after her mother. Kyle pulled on his jeans and made his way to the shower. After getting rinsed, he found some clean clothes and made his way to the kitchen. Rachel stood at the sink, her back to him, and the sight of her standing there, dressed in her work clothes with her hair tied back in a ponytail set his heart thumping. He clenched down on his jaw, calling on every ounce of strength he had not to go over there, turn her around and plant a warm, good morning kiss onto her mouth.

"Uncle Kyle, you can sit by me."

At the sound of his name, Rachel turned. Her eyes met his and he sucked in a breath. She looked warm, sexually sated and...sad. A smile touched her mouth, but it was forced.

She wiped her hands on the dish towel and tossed it over her shoulder. "Morning, sleepy head," she said, keeping things light. Good. Light he could handle. Ava giggled and he relaxed slightly. "Did you sleep well?" Rachel asked. "Was the bed comfortable?"

"You have a very comfortable bunk bed, Ava." He turned to the little girl, who was in pink princess pajamas. Then he winked and added, "Thank you for letting me sleep in it, but maybe tonight you can hook me up with a pillow."

"Oh, I'm sorry." Rachel's face turned a pretty shade of pink. "I never noticed...I mean I have an extra one on my bed you can have." She put a bowl in front of him, and he noticed the shakiness in her hand as she pointed to the box of cereal. "Help yourself."

Ava dug her spoon into her cereal and took a big bite. "Can we go see the dogs again today?" she asked around a mouthful of Cheerios.

"Ava," Rachel said. "We don't talk with our mouth full."

Ava put her hand over her mouth, chewed, and swallowed. "Can we go see the dogs again?" she repeated.

"That's better." Rachel smiled at her daughter.

"Sure, if you'd like. And maybe we could go to the pool. It's supposed to be a scorcher and a friend of mine works there. I'd like to say hello."

Ava clapped. "Yay! Are we going to work on the tree house too?"

"Yup, for a bit, but when it gets too hot we'll go swimming." Rachel poured him a mug of coffee and set it in front of him. Her hand accidently brushed his as she passed the sugar, knowing just how he liked it. Her warm scent drifted past his nose, and his body stiffened, memories from last night bombarding him.

"I don't have any cream, only milk," she said, sounding breathless.

"That's okay. Milk is fine." He dropped two sugar cubes into his mug, chased them with a spoon, then poured in a generous amount of milk. He took a much needed drink, hoping it would clear the lust from his brain. "Oh, Rach. I was talking to the guys last night at Sky Bar and we're invited to a barbeque at Matt's place this weekend. He passed his MCATs and is celebrating."

She frowned, and looked into the coffee pot. "I...I'm not...sure."

"Ava's invited too." He turned to Ava. "You remember Gemma from the shelter?"

Ava nodded. "She's nice."

"She is nice, and she's going to be there and she has a daughter your age."

"Can I go, Mommy?"

"We'll talk about it tonight." Rachel dropped a kiss onto

Ava's head. She turned to Kyle. "I'll be home around five. You know to call if you need anything."

"Yeah, but we'll be fine." He reached out and ruffled Ava's hair. "Right, squirt?"

"Right," she said.

He looked at Rach, who was staring at him, an emotion he couldn't identify dancing in her eyes as her hands squeezed the tea towel. "You okay?"

She blinked and took a small step back. "Yeah. Ava, be sure to wear your water wings at the pool."

"I will, Mommy."

Rachel left through the front door, and he dug into his cereal. When was the last time he'd had Cheerios? Ava began to chat on endlessly about her friend down the road and her new puppy. Since his brain was still functioning at half capacity from last night, he sat and listened, happy that she was so chatty because his mind was preoccupied with Rachel. What was that look she'd given him when he'd ruffled Ava's hair?

"If I had a dog, I'd walk it every day," Ava said, dragging his thoughts back.

So much for the tree house taking her mind off getting a dog.

He finished his cereal and his spoon clattered as he dropped it into the bowl. "What do you say we go to the compound first, then I have to make a trip to the hardware store. We'll come back for lunch and start on the tree house?"

"Okay." She jumped from her chair. "Mommy says I have to brush my teeth, wash my face, comb my hair and get dressed."

She put her bowl in the sink, and Kyle smiled as he watched her. James would have been so proud of her. Kyle washed up the dishes and put away the milk. On a plate inside the fridge he found three steaks defrosting, and it did the strangest things to him.

Ten minutes later Ava come running back in to the kitchen dressed in a pair of pink shorts and T-shirt with lollipops on it. She held out two elastic bands and a comb. "Can you do my hair again?"

Ugh. "Sure." He sat down and put her on his knees. She wiggled and shifted. Did she ever sit still? He dragged the comb through her hair, careful not to hurt her when he came across a few tangles.

"Ouch," she yelped. "That hurts."

"Sorry."

Ava clapped her hands and sang some patty cake song while he brushed out her hair and fumbled with the braids. He messed one up so badly, he had to start again.

She gave an exaggerated sigh when he started combing again. "Mommy does it faster."

"Cut me some slack. I'm new at this, squirt." Ava laughed and put her hands over her mouth. He twisted the hair, until he had what could pass for a pigtail. "I think my fingers are too big."

"You're silly," she said as he picked her up and set her back down on the floor. She shook her head, trying to see her braids.

"Ready?" he asked.

They left through the front door and Kyle fished his key from his pocket. He slipped it into the lock and Ava raced down the front steps without him. When he heard her squeal, he turned to find her running down the sidewalk.

Shit.

"Ava," he called out, his heart galloping. Where the hell was she going, and how could those little legs move so fast?

He went after her, but slowed his steps when he found her on her knees petting a puppy. Beside her was another little girl around the same age and he could only guess it was her friend, Lindsay, whose daddy had a job and the mommy stayed at home and walked the dog.

"Uncle Kyle," Ava said excitedly. "This is Muffin. She's so cute. I just love her." She picked the squirming puppy up and hugged it so tight, it's eyes practically bulged.

"Hello, Muffin." Kyle bent to pet the golden retriever pup.

When he stood back up, he found a very curious set of brown eyes looking at him. He held his hand out. "I'm Ava's uncle. Kyle Nelson."

"Nice to meet you, Kyle. I'm Shari Donovan, Lindsay's mom." She slipped her hand in his and as she shook, her gaze dropped to his chest, then lower. All righty then. If she was looking at him like he was a grade-A piece of meat and she'd just come off a vegetarian diet, then maybe Daddy who worked needed to be home a little more often. He pulled his hand back and shoved it into his pocket.

"I see the resemblance," she said. "She has your eyes."

"She has her dad's eyes," he corrected. "My brother."

"Oh." Her gaze narrowed, clearly putting the pieces together.

"Shari," a shrill voice called out from across the street. He angled his head to see two women out for their morning jog come running toward them.

"Hello there," the blonde in the yoga pants and matching black spandex top said.

"Did you move into the neighborhood?" the other lady asked as she pulled her hair from her ponytail and shook it out. The scent of floral shampoo reached his nostrils.

"This is Ava's uncle, Kyle," Shari said. "This is Audra and Krystal."

"Nice to meet you, Kyle." Audra stepped a bit closer. White teeth flashed in a smile. "Are you moving in, or passing through?"

He glanced at his niece. "I'm babysitting Ava for a couple weeks."

"Oh," Krystal said, stepping in front of her friend. "How lucky for Ava."

"I'm the lucky one. She's a great kid."

Krystal's eyes moved to his shoulders and he suddenly felt like a bug under the microscope. "Rachel never told us Ava had such a...strong uncle. Or that she had an uncle at all."

"What do you do, Kyle?" Audra nudged her way in front of Krystal. "I mean, besides babysit Ava."

"Army ammunition expert."

Audra bit her bottom lip, and sounding a little breathless she said, "So you blow things up."

"Something like that."

"How...dangerous." She twirled her hair around her finger. "Does it scare your wife?"

"I'm not married." Muffin barked and he was thankful for the distraction. "We should get going, Ava."

Krystal put her hand on his shoulder, her touch one-step past friendly. "Oh, so soon."

He moved back and her hand fell away. "Yeah, we have some things to do. Isn't that right, Ava?"

"We're building a tree house," Ava said to Lindsay. "Uncle Kyle, can I show Lindsay the tree house?"

He glanced at his watch, uncomfortable as three sets of eyes drilled in to him. "We need to get going but maybe she can come by later today."

"Can Lindsay come to the pool with us?"

Since he could barely keep up with one kid, he had no idea how he'd keep up with two, especially if Lindsay had Ava's energy. He hesitated, and Shari touched her friends on the shoulder to move them out of the way. They parted, and she stepped between them.

"I'd be happy to bring her there later," Shari said. "And if you'd like a lesson on how to braid hair I'd be happy to help. In fact if you need help with anything, anything at all, just let me know, okay."

"Yeah, okay." He reached down and captured Ava's hand. "Let's go."

"Bye, Lindsay." Ava hopped along the sidewalk beside him. He moved away from the women but could feel their gazes burning into his back. He popped the locks on the truck and helped Ava in. He turned and waved to the three women still watching.

Twenty minutes later, he pulled into the compound and shut the gate behind him. He helped Ava from the truck, and she jumped up and down and clapped when she saw all the dogs running around.

"Want to go play catch with Marley?"

She put her hand in his and he led her across the compound. When Marley saw them she came bounding over. She was a big dog, and as best as they could tell, she was a mix between a Saint Bernard and German Shepherd. She was a rescue dog. Some bastard had left her in a dumpster, and she was in pretty bad shape by the time she was taken to Gemma's shelter. What the fuck was wrong with people?

"Cuddles." Ava held her arms out wide.

Marley was sweet, but sometimes didn't know her own strength. She knocked Ava to the ground and stood over her, licking her face. Ava giggled and hugged the dog. "Oh, Cuddles."

"Easy, girl." Kyle pulled the dog off Ava and helped her to her feet.

"Come on, Cuddles," Ava said, and the dog responded, even though it wasn't her name. The two took off, and Ava found a ball. For the next half hour she played with the dog while he chatted with his comrades and helped carry lumber for the new training boxes they were making.

The sun was climbing higher in the sky by the time he settled Ava back in the truck. At first she didn't want to leave but he consoled her with building the tree house and swimming with her friend. She really did love dogs and it was too bad she couldn't have one. But he understood Rachel's reasoning. He'd love to have a dog himself but he was in no position to care for one.

"What do you want to have for lunch?" he asked.

"All my babysitters take me to McDonald's," she said.

Kyle laughed. "Oh, do they now?" She nodded, her pigtails bobbing around her face. "Something tells me your mom wouldn't like that."

"Mommy takes me there sometimes."

"How about we go for lunch at Sweetie's Bakery."

Her eyes widened. "Donuts!"

"We can get some to go. Your mom might like that." In fact he knew she would. When they were kids she could never say no to a chocolate-covered donut.

A short while later, after a quick trip to the hardware store, he entered the bakery. His stomach grumbled at all the delicious smells.

Ava took a big deep breath, and rubbed her stomach. "It smells good, Uncle Kyle."

"I know. It does."

He glanced around at the renovations Brad had done to his grandfather's old Victorian house. The main level had been converted into a bakery for his wife. He'd added on an outdoor wrap around deck, which was lined with small café tables, many of them occupied by the lunch crowd. The space was quaint, the perfect house for a bakery and to raise their family. Staff milled about, but in the back of the shop, he caught sight of Madison.

Ava in tow, he stepped up to the counter and said loudly, "What's a guy have to do to get some service around here?"

Madison spun around, and the second she set eyes on him, she came running over. She raced around the counter and gave him a big hug.

"Kyle," she said. He picked her up and spun her around. "What a nice surprise."

Her belly poked him and after he set her down he glanced at it. "I guess I'm not the only one with a surprise." He winked and added, "I hear it's something in the water."

She laughed and rubbed her stomach. "I guess you've been talking to Caleb. Just wait and see. Some girl will come along and he'll be reaching for a big glass."

He gave her a kiss on the cheek. "Seriously though, Madison. Congratulations. I couldn't be happier for you and Brad."

"I think Brad is hoping for a boy this time."

Madison stepped back and dipped her head. "And who is this beautiful young lady?" Kyle grinned at her. Madison knew who Ava was but guessed it had been a long time since she'd seen her. The last time was likely at James funeral two years ago.

Ava beamed, and reached out and grabbed Kyle's hand. "I'm Ava. Uncle Kyle is my uncle."

"Well, Ava." Madison put one hand on her hip. "How would you like to come to the kitchen and pick out something yummy? I just finished making a big batch of brownies."

Ava pulled her hand from his and put it in Madison's. He laughed at her switch of allegiances. Then again, he'd do the same if brownies were involved. "We have to have lunch first, Ava. Your mother would kill me if I let you eat a brownie first."

Madison's eyes turned serious. "How is Rachel?" she asked as he followed her around the counter to the back of the bakery.

"She's doing well. I'm hoping she'll come to Matt's barbeque on the weekend."

"We'd all love to see her."

Kyle's heart warmed. He loved how all his friend's worried and cared about Rachel. She'd been so busy with life that she'd obviously lost touch with everyone. Then again, it had been awhile since he hung out with his old friends, too and had to admit he really missed them. He missed home.

Ava watched in fascination as Madison showed her around the kitchen and gave her an eggbeater full of icing to lick. She then filled a box with donuts for her to take home to her mommy.

Madison glanced at her watch. "How about we all have lunch on the deck?"

"I don't want to take you away from your work."

"I only work half days, now. I like to spend the afternoons with Lexi."

"Who is Lexi?" Ava asked.

She tapped Ava on the nose. "My little girl."

"Does she have a daddy?"

Madison and Kyle exchanged an uneasy look. "She does," Madison said. "He's at work right now though."

"If I had a daddy, I could get a puppy."

On that note, he reached for Ava's hand. "Come on, Ava. Let's go look at the menu and see what you'd like to have for lunch."

Madison turned toward the staircase leading to her home upstairs. "I'll go get Lexi. Why don't you grab a table and Jessica will bring over some menus." She gestured toward the young girl behind the counter.

"Sounds great," Kyle said.

A few minutes later Madison returned with her daughter, Lexi, who was a spitting image of her mother. The four of them all sat at an outdoor table and enjoyed soup and sandwiches for lunch. Ava and Lexi hit it off instantly and sang songs as he caught up with Madison.

Soon good-byes were exchanged and he was on his way back to the house. With a box of donuts on her lap—she was keeping them close—Ava stared out the window and yawned.

"Tired, squirt?"

"Nope." She shook her head so hard, her pigtails flew in the air. "I want to work on the tree house and go for a swim."

"If you're tired you can have a nap."

"I'm too big to nap."

"Not me. I'd love to have one."

"You're silly," she said. "Mommy's going to like the donut I picked out for her."

"I'm sure she will." He pulled his truck into the driveway. "Home sweet home," he said, then stilled. What the hell? Christ, he'd only been here a couple days and he shouldn't be thinking about Rachel's place as his home.

He helped Ava from the truck and sent her upstairs to get changed into her work clothes. She came back sporting her coveralls, tool belt, and work boots.

"All ready," she said.

They went outdoors and he put her to work holding the measuring tape while he penciled off the cuts he needed to make. He explained everything he was doing, and how he planned to build the tree house low for her and her friends.

Hands on hips she listened carefully, excitedly then out of nowhere said, "Lexi said she is going to have a baby brother."

"That's right. Madison is having a baby."

"Can I have a baby brother too?"

"Well..." Shit, how the hell was he supposed to answer that one? "It's not that simple."

She went quiet. "It's 'cause I don't have a daddy, right?"

He set down the wood he was carrying and put his hands on her shoulders. "Ava, honey," he began having no idea how to field her question. "You have lots of people in your life. You have your mommy, your grandma and grandpa, and me."

She reached out and ran her hand along the lumber, then screeched. She jerked her arm away and started to cry.

His heart missed a beat as her face contorted in pain. "What is it?"

She jumped up and down, the tears spilling fast. "Ava, honey. Let me see your hand."

"No, it hurts."

He scooped her up and hurried in to the house. He set her on the kitchen counter and brushed her tears away. "You have to let me look, Ava." With the biggest frown he'd ever seen, she held her hand out. He examined her and felt a measure of relief to know it wasn't something serious. Of course, to Ava it was. "It's a splinter. I can take it out in a second."

She snatched her hand back. "No, it's going to hurt."

"I'll make it all better. I promise, okay?" He scooped her up, put her on his hip and darted upstairs. "Does your mommy have a first aid kit?"

She shook her head. "I don't know."

"Where does she keep her Band-Aids?" He rushed to the upstairs bathroom and rooted through the medicine cabinet, feeling a little strange going through her stuff. He found antibacterial ointment and bandages and set them by the sink. He turned back to Ava. "Where does Mommy do her makeup?"

Ava pointed to Rachel's bedroom. Kyle carried her down the hall and set her on Rachel's bed when he saw her makeup table. He peeked inside the floral cosmetic bag but his search came up empty. He looked at the bank of two drawers on each side, and while he felt a little uncomfortable going through her things, he had no choice.

He opened the top right drawer and rooted around, then turned his attention to the bottom one. Inside he found a stack of papers, and what looked like medical records. His heart missed a beat. Was Rachel sick? Unable to help himself, he pulled out the first paper and glanced over it. *Ava.* She'd had a series of medical tests done. He looked at the date, and exhaled a relieved breath when he saw it was from a couple of years back. Of course Rachel would have had her daughter genetically tested when James had died.

Something niggled at the back of his mind as he glanced over the paper one more time. With Ava whimpering behind him, he had no chance to think about it, so he put the paper back, and turned his attention to the bank of drawers on the other side. He opened the first one and found what he was looking for.

"These will work." He turned to find Ava watching him. Her hand was curled into a ball and she held it close to her chest.

He scooped her up and carried her back to the bathroom. "You're being so brave, Ava, that I think we should get into those donuts early," he said, trying to distract her. He grabbed the tip of the splinter with the tweezers. "Then we can go to the pool for a swim."

She whimpered as he tugged and pulled the splinter free. Blood pooled on the cut, and he washed it away.

She examined her finger. "It's gone."

"Now we'll put some ointment on it, and a bandage."

"Can I still go swimming?"

"Of course you can."

The doorbell rang and her eyes went wide. "Wait until I show Lindsay my cut."

*Wait until she showed her mother.*

"Hello," a voice said from below. "The door was open."

Ava squirmed to get free. He lifted her from the sink, and the second her legs hit the floor she was off and running. She hurried down the stairs and he followed to find Lindsay and

Shari standing in the kitchen. Ava proceeded to tell Lindsay all about her splinter, while he stood there feeling like a heel.

Shari blinked up at him. "It sounds like you had an eventful day." She held out a plate of muffins and cookies. "Maybe these will cheer you up."

"Thanks," he said. "You didn't have to do that."

"What kind of person would I be if I didn't welcome you to the neighborhood properly?" She clapped her hands. "So what do you say we all hit the pool?" She looked him over and nibbled her bottom lip. "You might want to put on a suit."

"Me too." Ava dashed back up the stairs.

"Don't forget your water wings," he called after her, proud of himself for remembering. "I'll be right back." He turned from Shari and followed Ava up.

Ava went to her room and he went to his. He stripped and tugged on his knee length suit. Ava came running from her room, the straps on her frilly purple suit all twisted.

"Wait, squirt," he said, and dropped to one knee. "You're all twisted."

"You're twisted." She giggled, cupped his face and kissed his nose as he fixed her straps.

His heart squeezed to the point of pain. Christ, he was in so much trouble. Not only was he in love Rachel, he was falling so damn hard for her little girl too.

number 7

"I missed you at lunch," Sara said, her high heel shoes clattering on the sidewalk as she hurried her steps to catch up to Rachel.

"Crazy busy day," Rachel explained, her eyes focused on her flats as she maneuvered around the crowd and walked down the busy sidewalk toward her car.

"Uh huh."

Rachel squeezed around a group of teens walking toward her and angled her head to see Sara's blue eyes glistening in delight as they stared at her. "What's that supposed to mean?" she asked, even though she wasn't so sure she wanted to hear the answer.

Sara pulled a pack of gum from her purse, pushed a piece through the plastic bubble and popped it into her mouth. "It means you took my advice." She held the pack out for Rachel.

Rachel shook her head, and as Sara studied her, she thought about lying. But there was no sense in denying it. Sara could always see right through her.

"That obvious, huh?" She slowed her steps outside a convenience store, utterly trumped.

"Sweetie, one look at you and I could tell you had sex last night."

"Shh." She glanced around to make sure none of the patrons entering or exiting the store had heard Sara. She lowered her voice. "What gave it away?"

Sara pursed her lips and circled her finger in front of Rachel's face. "The glazed look in your eyes, the way your skin is glowing. Those are all tells, but the biggest giveaway is in the way you're walking."

"What?" she said mortified as Sara laughed. "I was not walking funny," she shot back.

"You kind of were." She licked her lips. "He was big, huh?"

"Oh my God," she moaned and put her hands over her face as heat crawled up her neck.

Sara pulled her hands away and she looped her arm through Rachel's and started them walking again. "Nothing to be embarrassed about. You're both consenting adults."

"I know but—"

"No buts." Sara rubbed her hands together. "Now tell me everything."

Her mind took that moment to reminisce about the way he'd touched her with deft hands, taking her to places she'd never been before. Her skin still tingled from his kisses, burned from his hot mouth. Heat flooded her core, and she pressed her hand to her stomach. As a shudder raced through her, she pinched her lips tight, not wanting to share the intimate details with anyone yet.

"Well," Sara pressed.

"Well...I went to his room and it sort of happened." She paused and crinkled her nose. "I think."

"You think?"

"I don't know." She brushed her forehead, trying to make sense of it all. "Maybe on some level I went to his room with the intention of it happening." After all, she had worn her pretty panties.

"I know I would have." Rachel arched brow and Sara laughed. "Come on, the guy is smoking hot." Sara snapped her fingers. "I can't believe someone hasn't snatched him up already." Sara pulled her keys from her purse and hit the unlock button as they approached her car. "Interesting that he's not taken, don't you think?"

"Maybe, maybe not. Either way I probably shouldn't be having sex with him."

"Why not?"

"We've been over this."

Sara leaned against her car. "You want him, he wants you. What's the big deal?"

"The big deal is he's James's brother and after sex he told me we couldn't allow it to happen again." Plus, she was holding a huge-ass secret from him. Yeah, there was always that. But she couldn't tell Sara that. At least not before Kyle. And now, the longer she waited the harder it was becoming.

"So he has a loyalty to his brother. I get it. It's commendable. But seriously, wouldn't his brother rather you be with Kyle, a good man who will treat you right, than some random guy who could very well turn out to be an asshole? Trust me, there are a lot of them out there."

It was true. Sara wasn't the only one who'd come up against a few jerks. "I don't know. Even if you're right, I don't think Kyle would see it that way." He idolized his brother and happily stood in the shadows while James lived in the limelight. Everything he did was for his brother, which was why he was having a hard time letting go of the guilt and allowing himself to love. What happened between them last night was right. In her heart she knew they belonged together. Perhaps they always had.

Sara opened her car door and slid in. "Then you know what you have to do."

"What?"

"Make him see it that way. Show him how right you to are together."

"How?"

"You're a big girl and know Kyle better than anyone. You should be able to figure it out."

She nodded, understanding full well what her friend meant. "Are you going to Matt's this weekend for the barbeque?"

"Yeah, you?"

She gave a non-committal shrug. "Thinking about it."

"Come. It will do you good to get out. Everyone misses you, you know."

"I miss them too. I've just been busy."

"Rach," she said, her voice softer. "It's time to put yourself out there again, to get out and join the living. I know you always put Ava first, but your needs are important, too. If you don't start doing for you, you're going wake up one of these days and Ava will be grown up and gone, and you'll be all alone. Reach out to your friends, reach out to Kyle."

"Sara," she began cautiously. "Everyone knows Kyle is staying at my place, what would they think..." She let her words fall off. And what would they think of her when they found out about Ava, and that she'd kept the truth from Kyle.

Sara jumped from her seat, and pulled Rachel in for a hug. "They're your friends. They don't judge. Those who do, you don't need in your life."

She nodded, and with that last thought in mind, Sara jumped back in to her car and Rachel closed the door. With a little more spring in her step, she turned back around and hoofed it to the convenience store. She combed the aisles until she found what she was looking for. Then, waiting until there were no customers at the front counter to pay for her purchase. It was silly really. She was a grown adult and shouldn't be embarrassed, but the store was close to her work and she didn't want her coworkers to see her buying condoms. Better to have them on hand, than not...just in case.

The cashier rang her up and put her goods in a brown paper bag. She tucked her purchase under her arm and made her way to her car. She was anxious to get home, to see how Ava and Kyle's day went. Ava had been so excited to go see the dogs and spend the day with Kyle. It truly warmed her heart how much she'd taken to him. Not that it surprised her. They were after all, family.

A few minutes later she pulled into the driveway and could smell the barbeque. She grabbed her bag and darted around the back of the house to find Kyle at the barbeque and Ava sitting on the patio coloring. Her heart missed a beat as she looked them over, taking in their sunburnt skin.

She hurried up the stairs and Kyle gave her a sheepish look when she met his glance.

"I forgot the sunscreen." He gave her a pained smile. "But we did remember the water wings."

"Mommy, look." Ava dropped her crayon and held her bandaged finger out for Rachel to examine.

"Yeah, and there was a splinter too." He gestured to the steaks, his look so boyish and adorable it took her back in time. "But I made dinner," he added with an, "I hope I'm not in too much trouble and this gets me off the hook" look on his face.

She dropped to one knee and looked at Ava's pink shoulders, then checked her bandage. "Are you okay?"

"Uncle Kyle used tweezers. But I was brave, wasn't I, Uncle Kyle? And I got to have a donut."

Rachel cocked her head. "A donut?"

"Don't worry," Kyle piped in. "She had a healthy lunch." He laughed. "At least I got something right today."

"We got you a donut too, Mommy. We went to the bakery and had soup and sandwiches with Madison and Lexi."

"What fun." She gave her daughter a kiss on the forehead and was about to stand when Ava pointed to the bag.

"Mommy, what's that?"

She grabbed the bag tighter. With the burns and splinters, she'd forgotten to hide her purchase. "Oh, it's Mommy stuff," she explained then turned her attention to Kyle.

"Kyle—" she began.

"I'm sorry," Kyle said. "I feel pretty bad."

Her heart turned over, and she reached out and touched his hand. He flinched slightly as their fingers grazed, and she pulled her hand back.

"What I was about to say is don't be too hard on your-self." Truthfully, the man carried a lot of blame. Too much blame. She snapped her fingers. "With kids, accidents happen in the blink of an eye. Once Ava was standing on the sofa looking out the window. I was beside her and the next thing I knew, she fell backward and hit her head on the coffee table. I was right there, and it just happened."

He winced. "Was she okay?"

"A concussion, but she's okay now." She glanced at her daughter, her sweet, happy, healthy daughter. "And the burn isn't that bad. Yours is much worse." Her gaze moved over his forearms, stopping when she met the short sleeves of his T-shirt. She could only guess he'd been shirtless at the pool, and the burn covered his entire upper torso. "Let me grab the aloe."

"It can wait." He recapped the barbeque sauce. "Dinner is ready."

"I'll set the table. Just let me get out of these work clothes." She stepped inside and found a box of donuts along with three dinner plates loaded with cookies, muffins and squares. She picked one plate up, examined the sweets, then turned back around. "What's all this?"

Kyle glanced at her through the screen door. "Your friends welcoming me to the neighborhood."

What the heck? "Which friends?"

"Shari, Audra, and Krystal. I met them this morning, then again later at the pool."

She dropped the plate back down on the counter. It hit with a thud. "How very nice of them."

A surge of jealousy moved through her. How dare these women hit on Kyle? As she chewed on that a bitter taste settled on the tip of her tongue. She was about to dash upstairs to get changed and rinse her mouth when the reality of the situation stung like a slap. Honestly, why shouldn't they hit on Kyle? Well, save for Shari, who was married. He was hot, hard, sweet...*available*. If she was single and she'd seen him hanging out in the neighborhood, she'd probably do the same.

Wait! What?

She *was* single, and he wasn't just hanging out in the neighborhood, he was living in her house. Sure, he'd asked for friendship because of his loyalty to his brother. While having him as a friend was important to her, if she didn't do something right *now* to prove how right they were for each other, to help him let go of the guilt of the past, then she could very well lose him again. Nothing was stopping him from up and leaving again, walking straight out of hers—and Ava's—life like he did last time. Or, equally as bad, if she didn't do something soon, one of those women could get their claws in deep. She couldn't allow that to happen. She loved him too much.

The sound of Ava's voice drew her attention. Yes, she had a huge secret, but if Kyle realized how good they were together, then maybe, just maybe he wouldn't hate her for keeping it from him, or himself for his disloyalty. Maybe he could see that their daughter had been made out of love, not betrayal.

As she warmed to that idea, she darted up the stairs, placed her purchase into her nightstand, and slipped into a pair of jean shorts and a T-shirt. She pulled the elastic from her hair and reached for her brush. The bristles felt good on her skull after having her hair tied back in a tight ponytail all day.

She placed the brush back on her makeup table, her gaze going to her drawers.

*Uncle Kyle used tweezers.*

She pulled open her left hand drawer and rooted inside. No tweezers. A wave of unease hit as she sank down into her chair. Had he gone through her drawers in search of the tweezers? She checked her tabletop, moved the bottles of perfume around, but when the tweezers were nowhere to be found, she zeroed in on the bank of drawers to the right, to where she kept her very personal documentation.

Her fingers closed over the handle and she held her breath as she tugged it open. Inside she found everything in order, Ava's medical papers intact. If he'd found the documentation and read it, would the pieces fall in to place for him, or would he breeze over Ava's blood type and think nothing more of it?

A noise sounded at the door and she lifted her head but no one was there. The thought of him finding out before she had a chance to tell him spooked her more than she realized. Pushing away from the table she made her way to the bathroom, and found the tweezers and antibiotic ointment by the sink. Her heart twisted as she pictured Kyle bandaging Ava, his big hands so caring and gentle as he removed the splinter and applied the ointment.

"Mommy," Ava called from downstairs. "It's all ready."

"Coming." She shut the bathroom light off, took a breath to get herself together, then made her way down the stairs. Ava was setting the silverware on the table, while Kyle divvied up the meat and potatoes.

"Dinner is served," he said with a smile when he saw her. He placed the plates on the table and pulled three water glasses from her perfectly functioning cupboard.

"Kyle, this looks amazing. Thank you. I can't believe you even made a salad."

Mimicking Ava, he put his hands on his hips. "I was informed that something green must always be on the plate."

"I helped cut the cucumber," Ava said.

Rachel sat and grabbed the tongs. She put a generous amount of salad on each plate, then patted the chair next to her. "Ava, come sit and tell me all about your day." Her heart melted as Ava plunked herself down beside her. While she loved her job, some days she felt she was missing out on so much.

"Well, we went to see the dogs. I like Cuddles." She dug her fork into her potatoes and steam rose from it as she brought a big bite to her mouth.

"Who is Cuddles?"

Kyle shrugged, a smile tugging at the corners of his mouth as he reached for his fork. "Her name is Marley, but Ava calls her Cuddles for some reason."

"Is it because she's little and likes to cuddle?" Rachel asked as she cut in to her meat.

"No, Mommy, she's big." Ava held her hands out wide, then hugged herself. "But she likes to cuddle me."

Kyle laughed. "More like she likes to knock you to the ground and lick your face."

"Eww." Rachel crinkled her nose.

Ava giggled and stabbed at a piece of cucumber as she

fidgeted in her chair. "Then we went to see Madison and Lexi."

The last time she'd seen Madison was at James' funeral. "How is Madison?"

"She's doing great. She said business has tripled since moving. Brad did a good job on renovations. As soon as lunchtime hit, the place was packed. You should stop by and see her. She asked about you."

"Hopefully I'll see her at the barbeque."

"You're going to go?"

She nodded and Ava started clapping. "Yay, I get to play with Lexi again."

Rachel bit into her meat and moaned. So good. The man definitely knew his way around a barbeque. "It was nice of her to take the time off work to have lunch with you two, especially if she's as busy as you say."

"She only works half days," he explained.

"Oh, I didn't realize."

"Yeah, afternoons are spent with Lexi."

An invisible band tightened her heart. "That's nice." She wished she could do the same. But it didn't feel right for her to be living off James's inheritance. His folks already thought she was some sort of gold digger and she was hell bent on standing on her own two feet. But were they all suffering because of her stubbornness, her need to prove herself to her in-laws?

"Lexi is getting a baby brother," Ava said.

"What?" Rachel's fork stopped half way to her mouth. "Really? She's pregnant again?"

Kyle nodded. "I hear it's something in the water," he teased and set his glass down as she picked hers up. Coincidental?

"Yeah, Lexi is going to be a big sister. I want to be a big sister too." Ava went right on speaking over them, waving her fork around, as well as the piece of tomato dangling from the prongs. "Mommy, can I have a baby brother?"

Rachel nearly choked on her water and Kyle held his index finger up, his face contorting. "Uh, yeah, forgot to mention she asked about that earlier."

"Ava, sweetheart, it's not that simple. You need a mommy and a daddy for a baby."

Ava's eyes went wide, like a light bulb had gone off. "Mommy, why can't Uncle Kyle be my daddy? That way I can get a baby brother and a puppy!"

Her gaze met Kyle's and they exchanged a long, uncomfortable look as Ava squealed in delight. From her peripheral vision, she could see Ava's pigtails bobbing around her shoulders as she chewed her tomato and bounced in her seat like she'd just come up with the most perfect solution to all her problems.

Kyle broke eye contact with her and put his hand on Ava's. "That can't happen, squirt. I'm only here for a couple weeks. I'm leaving right after Easter, remember?"

She frowned, and planted her elbows on the table. "But—"

"No buts, Ava. Now take your elbows off the table."

They all went quiet for a long time, finishing their meals in silence, well, for the most part. Ava continued to fuss in her seat and talk about being a big sister as she made a nice dent in her food.

Kyle finally broke the silence between them. "How was your day, Rach?"

Rachel forced a smile. "Same old, same old. Lots of cleanings. I did find out the office is moving in a few weeks."

"Oh." He set his fork down and leaned back in his chair. "Where to?"

"Out in Westwood Hills. A bit longer commute than I

have now." She frowned. "Which means longer hours for Ava at the sitter."

"I know it doesn't help with that right now, but while I'm here I'd like to continue watching her. We still have a lot of work to do on the tree house. Don't we, squirt?"

She crinkled her nose at Kyle and giggled. "I'm going to have a tea party when we're done. Uncle Kyle, will you have a tea party with me and Lindsay?"

"A tea party. I thought we were going to drink beer and read super hero comic books."

She rolled her eyes. "I don't drink beer, silly."

Rachel's heart crashed against her chest as she listened to Kyle tease Ava, then when Kyle looked at her, she asked, "Are you sure?"

"Positive." He held his hand out for Ava to fist punch it but she looked at him in confusion. He reached for her hand and showed her how, then winked at Rachel. "I'll make a tomboy out of her yet."

God, she loved watching the two of them ham it up. Everything about them together was picture perfect. "You have your work cut out for you," she said with a laugh. But seriously, having him stay here at the house for the duration of his time home fit into her plan perfectly. If she were going to show Kyle how much they belonged together, then having him under the same roof would make it so much easier.

Ava took off to her room to play as they cleared the dishes together, she washed and Kyle dried. The normalcy in it all made her ache with a sense of longing and wanting exactly what Ava had so blatantly laid out earlier.

After the kitchen was cleaned, Kyle put the dish towel over his shoulder and turned to her. With only inches separating them, she could feel the heat of his body, the sexual tension arching between them. Need nipped at her stomach as she exhaled a shuddery breath.

"I'm going to head out to Sky Bar." He jerked his thumb toward the door. "Catch up with the guys."

"Okay, I'm going to give Ava a bath and tuck her in. Maybe we can dig out one of our favorite movies later. I still have *When Strangers Meet*."

He scoffed, and jabbed his thumb in to his chest. "*My* favorite movie. Yeah right. I only watched it six hundred times with you because..." His words fell off and a muscle in his jaw twitched as he whipped the tea towel off his shoulder and draped it around the stove handle.

"Because why?"

Her glance dropped to his backside and the way his jeans hugged his body so nicely. Her insides buzzed to life, and a quiver traveled from the top of her head right down to her toes. He turned but she was slow to react and when she lifted her gaze, he was staring at her.

He angled his head, opened his mouth, then closed it. When he finally spoke, he said, "Because James wouldn't." At the mention of his brother tension returned to his body. He twisted, grabbed his keys off the counter and walked to the screen door. "Don't wait up for me. I'm going to be late."

"Oh, okay." Disappointment moved through her and he must have sensed it.

He spun back around, and his shoulder dropped. "Rach," he whispered, taking a small step closer.

"Yeah." He reached out to her, and one strong hand closed around her shoulder. Heat reverberated through her blood as the rough pad of his thumb brushed over her collarbone. A gentle caress that said how much he needed her. She knew the feeling well.

Her heart sped up, the pull between them undeniable. But he was fighting it and somehow got it into his head that he was the one responsible for everything happening between them, the one taking advantage of her. She needed to show him that that wasn't the case at all. She could tell him, of course. Tell him they were both in this together, that she wanted this as much as he did, but he likely wouldn't believe her.

What if she made the first move...?

His gaze dropped to her mouth, and she caught the hungry gleam in his eyes. Anticipation moved through her as she listened to his throat work. Was he going to kiss her again, to finally let himself love? His Adam's apple bobbed, as if going down for the third count.

"Kyle?"

"I'm going to take off," he said. "I'll see you later."

He exited through the back door, like he couldn't get away quick enough. His truck revved to life as Ava came running in to the kitchen.

"Where is Uncle Kyle going?"

She sucked in a quick breath to pull herself together. Plastering on a smile, she turned to her daughter. "To visit friends, and that gives us some quiet time together." She scooped Ava up. "So come on. Bath time." She tapped a squirming Ava on the nose. "Then, we can read." She carried her little girl to the foot of the stairs then set her down on the floor with an exaggerated breath. "You're getting too big for me to carry."

Ava darted up the stairs ahead of her and she watched her go. She wished she could give the child everything she wanted, especially a sibling. As an only child herself, she'd been lonely growing up and wanted her daughter to have what the Nelson boys had. With only eighteen months between them the two had been so close, the bond between them strong. Ava was four already, and was going to miss out on creating such a connection. Unless of course, she could help Kyle let go of the past and accept everything he had in front of him, everything she and Ava had to offer. Then again, he hadn't wanted to drink the water. Maybe he didn't want this. One thing she knew for certain though, was she had to try. If she did nothing, and let him just walk out of her life again, she'd spend the rest of her days regretting it.

She followed Ava up the steps and ran the bath. Ava stripped off and started talking about Cuddles and babies as Rachel filled the tub with bubbles and helped her in. Rachel gave her a bath, then bandaged her finger after drying her off. She tucked Ava in bed and grabbed her favorite bedtime story from the bookshelf.

In minutes Ava was fast asleep. No doubt from the busy day with Kyle. Feeling a little too keyed up to go to bed herself, Rachel picked up her favorite romance novel and read as she took a long soak in a hot bubble bath. Darkness had fallen over the city by the time she climbed out, wrapped herself in a towel, and walked to her bedroom. She pulled open her dresser and looked over her nightclothes. The slip of silk material that one could barely call a nightgown drew her attention. She'd bought it on Sara's insistence last year when it was on sale but had no reason to wear something so pretty and slinky to bed alone. A nightgown like this was worn for one reason and one reason only. To be removed by hands other than her own.

She glanced at herself in the mirror over her makeup table. She turned sideways, taking in her curves and the way the soft material fell over her body. Would Kyle like it? Would it have the effect she was hoping for? Nervousness moved into her stomach as she wandered through the house. Why did it suddenly seem so empty without Kyle in it? Needing something to occupy her hands, she picked up Ava's toys and tidied up. When all was clean she made her way to her bed, and reached for the novel she'd been reading.

As the minutes ticked by the words before her blurred, and she found herself reading the same passage numerous times. It was hard to focus when she had a seduction planned. It was more than a seduction really. She needed Kyle to let go, to come undone, because only then could she help put him back together again and see things for what they were.

She glanced at the clock and sat up straighter at the sound of his truck pulling into the driveway. Easing the covers off, she listened for his footsteps on the staircase. They creaked beneath his feet and when she heard him on the landing, she drew a breath, and inched open her door to see him slip in to the bathroom. The shower turned on and she paced her room, waiting to make her move. Doubt crept into her thoughts. What if he turned her away and bolted?

What if he didn't?

The bathroom door opened and when she heard him hurry to his room, she stepped into the hall, stopping to grab the aloe from the bathroom.

Shuffling sounds could be heard in his room, and when the bedframe squeaked, she knocked softly. At first he didn't respond. Was he going to ignore her? Not wanting to wake Ava, she knocked again, a little harder this time, and called out to him.

"Kyle," she whispered.

His feet shuffled on the floor, and his door opened. Looking rugged and sexy, she found him standing before her in nothing but a towel. Unable to help herself, her glance left his face and traveled down his body, taking pleasure in his tanned skin stretched tight over muscles carved to perfection. She ached to caress him again, to lose herself in the warmth of his touch. He cleared his throat and her gaze returned to his.

"Hey," she murmured.

"Hey," he returned, his voice sounding strained as his heated gaze swept across her. There was a new intensity about him that made her nerves jump. "What's up?"

"I forgot to give you the aloe vera." He continued to stare at her, like he had no idea what she was talking about. "You know, for the burn." She held the bottle up for him to see and took in the hard angles of his face, his suntanned skin, and strong jaw. And then there was his mouth. Soft, sensual, capable of giving so much pleasure. Heat curled through her and her cheeks flushed hotly. There was something undeniably primal about this rough and rugged soldier that teased and tortured the woman in her. She let out a fluttery breath and pointed to his broad chest and six pack. "I was just checking out your burn."

He relaxed a bit. "Oh, right."

"It's still bad, you should put this on." He reached for bottle but she pulled it away. "It's okay, I can do it."

He hissed air as she uncapped the lid and poured the lotion into her hand. Her glance moved over his chest again and as she reached out to place her palm on his body, he grabbed her wrist to stop her. His rough calluses scraped erotically against her skin as he held her still. She lifted her head, and the air crackled with sexual tension when his eyes met hers.

"Don't," he bit out, his nostrils flaring like he was in agony.

She blinked up at him. "What's wrong?"

He shook his head, a nervous energy about him as the blue in his eyes deepened. "I can't have you touching me like this again, Rach."

"Why not?"

"Because the last time you put lotion on me... well...I took..."

"*We* took." She planted her pelvis next to his, and the tell-tale hardness between his legs told her he wanted this—her— as much as she did. "*We* fell into that bed together." Why couldn't he see that they were both responsible for what happened? That he wasn't taking advantage of some vulnerable girl, or betraying anyone.

His jaw clenched. "We're not going to fall in to it again. We can't."

"Okay." She captured his hand and gave a little tug.

"What are you doing?" he asked. She pulled him into her room. His entire body stiffened at the sound of her lock clicking into place. His glance went from her, to her unmade bed, back to her again. He opened his mouth to speak but no words came.

Taking the lead she said, "How about we fall into mine?" She lifted her chin, parted her lips and swiped her tongue over them in invitation.

Eyes, dark and needy, pulled away from hers and for a moment she thought she lost him. But then his breathing changed, became rough as he zeroed in on her mouth.

"Rach... Fuck... I..." He brushed his thumb over her cheek, his touch so caring and gentle it took her breath away.

"You what?" she asked.

"I...I need...I fucking need, okay."

"Then take."

**8**

"Take what you need, Kyle." Her hand went to his chest, the soothing balm in her palm cool on his heated skin. His cock surged to life. "Take what you need and give me only what you can give." She massaged gently, and he closed his eyes in distress as she rubbed the ointment over his body.

As need warred with loyalty, he strove to pull himself together, to get out of her room before he did something he knew he'd regret later. Feeling a little shaky, unstable, he called on every ounce of strength he possessed and made a move to go, but stopped dead in his tracks when she spoke.

"I want you," she murmured, her voice soft, seductive. The way she looked at him with such need and desire, such honesty and openness complicated his mission to keep his distance. Jesus, he was weak, so fucking weak when it came to her. "I want you in my bed. I want you inside of me."

His hand shook as he closed it over hers to stop her, but the heat from her fingers felt so goddamn good, all he wanted to do was sink to his knees and drag her down with him. He took in the creamy rise of her breasts and as her breathing changed, became irregular, it nearly shut down his brain. How the fuck could he be expected to stay strong when she had such perfect breasts, nipples? He grabbed a fistful of his hair and tugged as the air around them grew heavy, charged with sexual energy.

"Rach..."

His voice fell off when she stepped back, giving him an unhindered view of her see-through nightgown. As she moved, she dragged his focus with her, and the sight nearly took him to his knees. Unable to rein in his lust, he looked his fill, taking pleasure in her beautiful, pale nipples as they poked through the slip of material. He clenched down on his jaw hard enough to break bone as his mouth watered for a taste. Christ, the woman was whittling away what little control he had.

The towel around his waist tented and he angled his body, but there was no fucking way he could conceal his growing erection. Her gaze dropped, and the longer she stared at his bulging towel, the thicker he grew.

"Tell me you don't want this," she said softly, her gaze traveling back up to meet with his. Dark eyes locked on his, and for a moment he couldn't breathe. "Tell me you don't want it and I'll walk away."

He could tell her, but it would be a total fucking lie. Impatience thrummed through him, blood rushing to his cock as the situation escalated beyond his power to stop it. She put her hand on her throat, and let her fingers trail downward. He followed the sexy movement and in the span of a second his brain shut down as the woman he loved, the woman he couldn't say no to, seduced him into her bed.

"Tell me, Kyle." When his name rolled off her tongue, heat arced between them, and the last of his resolve melted away. He resisted the urge to wave as logic packed a bag and headed south.

As she cut the leash holding him back he took two measured steps to close the distance between them. "I want this." Her breath shuddered as he moved into her personal space, standing so close the heat emanating off her body seeped under his skin and stirred all the things he felt for her.

He wrapped one arm around her waist and, ignoring the clanging bells in his head, he did the one thing he shouldn't do—crushed her body to his. His actions weren't rational, or smart, but fuck, when was the last time he made a good decision when it came to her?

Heat flooded him as his cock pressed against her stomach. Her dark lashes fluttered as she moved against him, rubbing his girth in a suggestive way. Fuck. He toyed with the thin strap on her nightgown, running his finger along it, under it, brushing her skin as he considered the buttons lining the front and how he'd like to disrobe her. One quick rip? Or slow and gentle? Tension grew in his body as he visualized the former.

"I want you so fucking much I can't even think straight when I'm around you." He laughed, but it came out sounding maniacal. "What the fuck am I talking about? I can't think straight even when I'm not around you."

"Take, Kyle."

His lips crashed down on hers, and as soon as he tasted her sweetness he knew he was done for. Craving the feel of her against him, he drew her tongue into his mouth and kissed her hard. Starved for so much more than a quick hurried orgasm, and wanting to give her so much more in return, he swept his tongue against the side of her mouth, savoring every inch of her.

Sweet. So fucking sweet.

She reached out and untied his towel. It fell to the floor and her hands raced over him in aroused eagerness. Her fingers slid lower and she wrapped her warm palms around his throbbing cock. He broke the kiss and sucked in a breath as her throaty purr resonated through him. Her hands glided over the length of him and when his whole body trembled her lips turned up at the corner. Jesus Christ, she liked it when he came undone—liked doing this to him.

He pulsed in her palms as she stroked him. So good. So fucking good. Pleasure forked through him and a low growl of longing sounded in his throat. He slid his fingers through her hair and cupped the back of her head as beads of moisture broke out on his flesh.

Her mouth moved to his neck, her soft lips like fire on his skin. She kissed a path downward, the heat of her tongue enough to drive any sane man mad as she explored his body.

"I want to taste you," she whispered against his skin, her lashes tickling his flesh. "Everywhere."

Fuck no. If she put that sweet mouth of hers around his cock, he'd go off like a damn cluster bomb. He couldn't let that happen, because he needed tonight to last so he could explore her body and hope to get his fill of her once and for all.

He gripped her shoulders to stop her exploration, and when her eyes snapped up, he leaned forward and ran his tongue across her bottom lip. Heaven. There was no other word to describe her taste.

"Me first," he said.

A little nudge set her into motion and he backed up until she was pressed against the wall. He grabbed her hands, removing them from his cock, and drew them over her head. He pinned them with one hand as he took full possession of her body with his mouth. His lips moved over her eyes, nose, jaw, and slid to her neck. He licked the sensitive spot that made her quiver.

"Kyle," she murmured, her soft whisper falling over him as she writhed. He looked at her. Eyes full of urgent need stared back. She was so fucking beautiful. A bevy of emotions crashed against his chest no matter how hard he tried to keep them at bay.

He cleared his throat. "Keep your hands there," he said, and inched away. He scrubbed his hand over his chin, the rasp of his whiskers cutting the quiet as his glance slid over her. His hands went to the buttons on her nightgown.

"Are you very fond of this?" He fingered the silky material.

"Not really," she said her chest rising and falling. "I've never worn it before."

His hand stilled and he clenched down his jaw. Tenderness moved through him, squeezing his heart and making it difficult to breathe. "You wore this for me," he said, a statement, not a question.

"Yes."

He ran his palms over the small buttons, starting at the top and stopping when he reached the juncture between her legs. He let his hand linger there, purposely nudging her clit, so desperate to give her pleasure. A little whimper escaped her lips.

"So in a sense, it's mine to do with as I please, then?"

Her pupils dilated. "Yes," she whispered.

"Good."

Giving in to impulse, he gathered the front of her nightgown in both hands and gave a quick tug. His heart slammed and lust gripped his cock at the surprised little *O* on her mouth. Her buttons scattered to the floor, and the excitement dancing in her eyes as he tore her clothes from her body fucked him over in ways he didn't know possible. His gaze traveled from her face to her breasts, to the juncture between her legs. If it weren't for the tightening of his throat, he would have sobbed with pleasure.

"No panties," he managed to get out as her gown spilled wide open, giving him an unobstructed view of her lush body.

His heart nearly failed as he gazed at her. The sight of her naked, up against the wall, waiting for him to touch her, to take her, robbed him of his next breath.

Everything about her was perfect. So goddamn perfect.

He hadn't thought it was possible to be more turned on than he was moments ago, but as she stood there, her body quaking under his inspection, his cock hardened and thickened to the point of pain. His dick wanted in, and it wanted in now.

"Take it off," he ordered. "Then put your hands back above your head."

Trust shimmered in her eyes as she lowered her arms and let the nightgown fall to the floor, and it did something strange to him. Without question, she lifted her arms again, completely baring herself to him. As she offered her body, opening herself up completely, he closed his eyes in sweet agony. How was it possible that seeing her like this, so unguarded, exposed, and trusting made him love her all that much more?

She whimpered and his eyes opened. He stepped into her, kicked her nightgown away and put his hands on either side of her head.

"I'm going to fuck you so hard tonight, Rach."

"Oh God," she cried out. She swiped her tongue over her bottom lip and he struggled to get himself together.

"But first I'm going to run my tongue all over you. Then, just when you think you can't take it anymore, I'm going to slip between your legs and take your pussy into my mouth."

Her cheeks turned a darker shade of pink and her warm breath washed over his face as she began breathing harder. "Then what?" she asked. He bit back a grin, loving the excitement, anticipation in her eyes.

"Then I'm going to lick you, a soft, slow slide of my tongue at first, all the way from the bottom to the top. Then

I'm going to increase the pressure and flick your clit with the tip. As you hover on the edge, I'm going to dip a finger inside you and fuck you with it until you can't think straight."

He slid one hand down her body, shaping her curves. He found her thighs, and shoved his hand in between. "Now open for me."

Heat suffused her body as she widened her legs, giving him full access so he could do as he pleased. His balls tightened. If he didn't get his mouth on her soon, he was sure to detonate.

"You are so fucking beautiful," he murmured, need making his voice husky as his fingers moved closer and closer to her center. Desire seared his insides when her heat reached out to him. Her passion-imbued eyes caressed him with sultry need and she rolled her hips forward, seeking relief.

He watched, transfixed as she moistened her mouth and, unable to help himself, he dipped his head and swiped his tongue over her bottom lip before pulling it between his teeth. He tugged gently and she made a sexy noise. He released her mouth and pressed his nose into her neck, breathing in her skin.

She visually quaked and his heart picked up tempo. He trailed his tongue lower and his fingers parted her nether lips, where he found her wet and swollen and so goddamn needy for him. Finding her like this made him crazed, wild with the need to forego the plan he'd just laid out and bend her over the bed so he could pound into her. Long, hard strokes that would leave his mark on her and show her how fast she could make him come undone. Wouldn't she like that? But he needed to take it slow, needed this night to last.

"Tell me what you want," he said his mouth so close to her nipple he could see it trembling, see how much it ached to be sucked. He circled her clit with the rough pad of his thumb, coming perilously close but never touching. Her hips came off the wall, trying to force his mouth to her breast, his finger to the spot that needed it most.

"I want you," she said, the words tumbling out in a rushed breath. "All of you."

He put his hand on her stomach and pushed her back against the wall. Restless, edgy as raw need camped in his groin, he skimmed his tongue over the upper swell of her breast. She groaned in frustration as he toyed with her, dragging out the seduction.

"Kyle, please," she begged.

"Is this what you want, baby?" Pretending to have some semblance of control, he found her nipple, and ran his tongue over her pillowed softness. It swelled in response, forming a tight peak that begged to be sucked and nibbled. He pulled one in and bit down until she cried out. Her hands went to his hair and she held him there, showing him what she needed, what she craved.

While he couldn't give her all of himself like she'd asked, tonight he could at least give her his body. He could fill her with his cock and take her to where she so desperately needed to go.

Her hands left his hair and went to his shoulders. She lightly scraped her nails over him, and her touch sent shockwaves through his nerves. Fuck, she was killing him.

With need ruling his actions, he dropped lower, pressing his mouth to her flesh and licking a path down her stomach. He twirled his tongue around her belly button and she arched into him.

Once again he pressed his hands to her hips and pushed her against the wall, needing her still so he could take his fill.

"You're so wet, baby," he murmured, letting his warm breath fall over her moistness. Her sex quivered and glistened in the lamplight. He widened her with his tongue and pressed a kiss over her pussy as his thumb applied pressure to her clit.

"Yes!" she cried out, and he looked up to find her watching.

He flattened his tongue and ran it from bottom to top, reveling in her sweetness. She moved against his mouth, her body seeking what it needed. Blinding pressure roared through him as his cock screamed for action. He removed his finger and flicked his tongue over her clit, and she moaned. He glanced up again to find her cupping her breasts and he just about shot off then and there.

"Fuck," he murmured, turning his attention back to her pussy. Her sweet scent assailed his senses, the cacophony of noises catching in her throat pushing him closer and closer to the edge of sanity.

He dipped a finger inside her, and when she clenched around him, he crooked it. Her entire body trembled as he brushed her sensitive bundle of nerves, knowing exactly where they were and exactly how she liked to be touched. There was nothing about her he'd ever forgotten.

She ground her pussy against his face. "Kyle, yes, like that. Just like that."

He pushed another finger inside her and pressed his mouth to her clit, kissing her hungrily. He pumped into her and lapped at her swollen nub, keeping up the rhythm until her entire body quaked.

"Yes," she cried out, as she gave herself over to the pleasure. "Oh God. Yes."

He loved seeing her like this, loved making her come. Her muscles squeezed his fingers, and the honeyed nectar on his tongue as he lapped at her nearly shattered his last vestige of control. The need to be inside warred with the need to taste every sweet drop. He stayed between her legs longer, his tongue gently stroking her sex as she rode out the waves.

When she stopped spasming, he slid back up her body and reached out to find her hands trembling. He pulled her away from the wall and walked backward, keeping her body tightly pressed against his. His cock rubbed her stomach, and when she put her arm around him and wiggled, massaging his throbbing appendage, he nearly ejaculated.

"Stop it." He reached behind her and gave her a whack on the ass. "If you don't I'm going to lose it." Her eyes went wide, but it was from excitement not fear. She wiggled again, and he cursed under his breath. "That's what you want, isn't it? For me to lose it." He sat on the bed and slid his hands around her body. He gave her ass another soft slap as he buried his face in her stomach, indulging in the softness of her skin.

She ran her hands over his shoulders, palming his muscles. "What I want is you, Kyle. All of you."

With his libido in an uproar, he stood, turned her around and fell over her as he shoved her down onto the bed. A gasp caught in her throat as he pressed her into the mattress, pinning her with his body. He put his hands on either side of her head and kissed her hard, their tongues tangling as he widened her legs to position himself in between. Her body softened beneath his, her hands on his body so needy. He went back on his knees, his muscles trembling as he grabbed her thighs and put them around his waist, shoving a pillow under her ass to lift it.

She looked so sexy laying here, her wet, hot pussy on display—his for the taking. As her body called out to him, begging for his touch, his cock throbbed in his hand as he leaned forward to run it over her clit. She went up on her elbows to watch, and he could sense her excitement. It matched his own.

"You like that, baby?" he asked, sinking in to her sensual warmth. Need sang through his veins as he ran the tip of his cock between her soft folds, rolling his crown around her clit until she was panting and clawing at him for more. Christ, his dick ached to push into her. "You want my cock? You want me to drive it all the way up inside you and fuck you hard?"

She trembled and nodded rapidly. "Condom," she whispered. "Nightstand."

He stilled. Christ, he'd been so lost in her he'd almost forgotten protection. As that realization slammed in to him, something niggled at the back of his mind, but he lost all train of thought when she closed her hand over his and centered his crown on her clit. Her eyes rolled as she stimulated herself and rocked her hips into him. She was so sexy and he loved how aroused she was, but if he didn't put a stop to this he was going to climax all over her.

With lust ruling, he pulled her hand away and fell over her. Stretching his arm, he reached into her nightstand and found a mega box of condoms. It was new, hadn't been opened. Was this what she'd been hiding earlier? Did she have this seduction planned all along? He let out a breath. He might be a hard-ass soldier, but honest to fuck, when she came at him with this kind ammunition, he was powerless to fight it.

He ripped into the foil with his teeth and was about to put it on when she stopped him. "Here, let me."

He threw his head back and growled. "Why is it you have to do everything? First the muscle rub, then the aloe vera, and now this. I'm seeing a pattern."

She laughed, a deep throaty sound that settled into his groin. "I like touching you." She pressed the condom to his crown, and his cock jumped.

*Fuck me.*

He fisted his hands. "Do you have any idea how hard that is on me?"

"Oh, yes, it's very hard," she said, amusement in her voice.

He scrubbed his chin as she slowly rolled it down his

length, her fingers stroking, burning his flesh. A surge of warmth stole through him.

"When you touch me, Rach. When you put your hands on my body, it makes me crazy."

"Crazy is good," she whimpered and fell back onto the bed, lifting her arms above her head to grab the slats in her headboard. Sweet Jesus. He loved seeing her like this, all wide open and ready, but this time he needed her on top, needed to see her when she came.

A sense of urgency overwhelmed him as his hands spanned her waist. In one fluid moment that seemed to take her by surprise, he rolled, taking her with him. Her light body settled on top of his, her beautiful nipples pressed against his chest and he trembled with need. Shaky hands tapped the sides of her legs.

"Up."

She bent her knees and lifted herself until she was straddling him from above. Never having felt so much desire for anyone, he touched her cheek, then ran his thumbs over her beautiful pale nipples. She moaned and leaned into him. The pleasure in her eyes rattled him to his core and touched him in places so deep, it was all he could do to keep it together.

Driven by need, he gripped her waist and lifted her, positioning his cock at her hot opening. She squirmed but he held her, offering her an inch at a time. He lowered her slowly, and as he pushed into her warm, wet heat, he closed his eyes in surrender. There was nowhere else in the world he wanted to be, and no one else he'd rather be with.

As her pussy muscles gripped him, he tightened his hands on her waist and pulled her down hard, driving all the way inside. She gasped as his fullness stretched her and he stilled to give her a minute to catch up.

"You good, baby?"

A quick breath, and then, "Yes." She rocked into him, leaning forward to brush her clit over his pelvis.

He let her ride him for a minute, then lifted her from his cock, only to slam back into her. She cried out his name as he continued to power his hips upward...needing...just needing. He pounded hard and fast, as he greedily took everything he needed.

A storm rolled through him as her breasts bounced and he sat up to take one hard nipple into his mouth. She threw her head back and cried out in sweet bliss as he sucked and bit. Christ, there was nothing gentle in the way he was taking her. Feeling ravenous, carnal completely out of control he fell back down onto the mattress, grabbed her hips harder and drilled into her.

His breath came jagged and she grew slicker with each stroke. Tightness settled in his groin, and as need consumed them both, their moans of pleasure blended. She cupped her beautiful breasts as he put one hand between their bodies to tease her clit. She rubbed up against his thumb with each downward motion.

He was so fucking close. She rode him harder and pressure built, coming to a peak. But he held on because he needed her to come, needed to see her face, her eyes, when she let go for him. The world closed in on him, and as she flew higher and higher, the desire in her eyes touched his soul.

"So good, Kyle. So good." She rotated her hips, taking him in deeper as she chased an orgasm.

Seeing her like this and knowing he could bring her so much pleasure, bolstered his ego. He jerked his hips, giving her every last inch. "That's it, baby. Take what you need." Her lids fell shut, and his heart raced. "Look at me. I need to see you when you come."

Her eyes opened and the second they locked on his, he

pressed harder against her clit. She threaded her fingers through her hair, a sexy sound catching in her throat as her muscles gripped his cock hard.

"Kyle," she cried out as she released all over him, her warm cream coating his cock. His balls found shelter inside his body and white-hot lightening flashed in his groin with the approach of his own orgasm.

Blood pulsing hot, he sucked in a tight breath and grabbed her hips to still her. He jackknifed up, buried his face in her neck and let go, his ejaculation sending ripples onward and upward through their bodies. A deep, satisfying growl rumbled in the air, the sex so good even his toes curled. Her sex muscles squeezed his cock, drawing out his orgasm until he was sated, too spent to think straight. Her hands went around his shoulders and he gripped her hair, giving it a little tug to expose more of her long neck.

When the last drop was spilled, he gasped for breath, moisture sealing them as one as he struggled to refill his lungs. She whimpered softly when he inched back and kissed her chin, her mouth, and her cheek. Without pulling out of her, he fell back and dragged her down with him.

Once he regained the ability to speak, he said, "Jesus, that was good."

She relaxed on top of him, her breath hot and harsh on his skin. "Kyle," she whispered, a slight hitch in her voice. The hot dampness on his neck filled him with unease. Fuck, was she crying? Had he hurt her?

He cupped her head and lifted it. When he saw the tears in her eyes, his gut squeezed. A sucker punch wouldn't have hurt as much. "Baby, are you okay?"

"I'm okay. I just...that was so beautiful." She pressed a soft kiss onto his mouth and rested back on his chest. Tenderness stole over him and his heart raced, ached to the point of pain as it filled with all the things he felt for her.

He stayed inside her and held her tight. He couldn't bring himself to let her go, was unwilling to break the connection between them. They both held on to one another like their lives depended on it, like if either let go they'd shatter into a million tiny pieces. A long while later, after his cock grew flaccid, he rolled to his side and eased out of her.

He discarded the condom and fell back onto her bed. His heart crashed against his chest and, entirely lost in the moment—in her—he drew her to him, wanting only to hold her, kiss her, and possess her. They'd crossed a line again, but he was powerless to resist her. He needed this as much as she did.

She put her hand on his chest and silence reined for a long time as he stared at the ceiling. He was in trouble, so much trouble when it came to her.

"I leave after Easter," he said, breaking the quiet. "I'll be gone for months."

She pulled back an inch but he cupped her elbow and held her to him. "I know." Her voice was soft, sad, a mere whisper.

He turned to her, and a pressure squeezed the center of his chest as she looked at him, her expressive eyes wary, worried. He kicked himself, her vulnerability slicing into him like a dagger. Christ, after the two last times they'd come together intimately what the hell did he expect? Twice now he'd pushed her away after lovemaking, practically tossing her out like she meant nothing to him. She blinked and lowered her gaze.

"Hey." He touched her chin and lifted it until her eyes met his. He held her face between his palms and his throat tightened when their gazes collided. Christ, sometimes it hurt just to look at her.

Rachel. Sweet Rachel who seduced him into her bed and asked for it all. Resisting her was fucking impossible.

He trailed his hands down her arms, caressing the soft

outer edges of her breasts. He dipped a hand between her legs and emotions churned inside him as he cupped her warm sex. When she moaned and pressed against him, he nearly lost all train of thought. Her sexy sounds penetrated his defenses. It was a mistake to take her again. A beautiful fucking mistake that never should have happened. But it did happen, and now they had no choice but to go forward from here.

"This," he began. "This is what I can give you until I leave, Rach. But it's all I can give."

Her hand moved to his cheek, and he leaned into her palm. As emotions played across her face, a wave of possessiveness overcame him. "Okay," she whispered, her mouth closing over his, her lashes fluttered against his skin as she cuddled in to him. "If it's all you can give, it's all you can give," she whispered.

She kissed him with such passion and need that when he finally broke away, it left him shaken. His heart squeezed because he wanted to give more. He truly did. Everything about this felt right. But it was wrong. Wrong on so many fucking levels.

## 9

Kyle stirred the pancake batter as Ava combed the hair on her doll. "If I had a real baby brother, I would comb his hair too," she said. "And if I had a dog, I'd comb her hair."

"So you want a boy baby and a girl dog?" Kyle stole a quick glance at Ava over his shoulder. He turned back and grabbed a frying pan from under the cupboard.

"I like Cuddles and she's a girl."

Even though he had his back to the room, the second Rachel entered it he knew. The hairs on his body prickled, and his heart pounded harder. Every instinct he possessed urged him to turn around, drag her into his arms and give her a warm, morning kiss. He brushed his arm over his forehead and worked to keep it together in front of Ava. But seriously, what that woman could do to him without even trying was baffling.

She stepped up to him, put her hand on his back, and leaned over his shoulder. He caught the intoxicating scent of her shampoo, the same fragrance she'd been using since their teens—and just like that, it whittled away what little control he had. Desire swept over him, and he forced himself to breathe.

Her nipples pressed against his back as she went up higher on her toes. "What's all this?" she asked, her warm, minty breath falling over his neck and settling in his groin.

A slight tug and she lifted his shirt. Her hand slipped underneath, and the softness on his skin nearly shut down his brain. He turned to face her and caught the warm, sated look on her face. Her hand slid around his body, going from his back to his stomach. There was a gleam in her eyes as her fingers lingered there, tracing his muscles and sliding along the top band of his jeans. Christ, she was touching him on purpose, knowing full well what it did to him. He shook his head at her antics. Dammed if she wasn't going to pay for this.

"I heard Ava get up, so I got up with her," he explained, hoping his voice came out sounding somewhat normal as her fingers stroked softly. "I thought I'd take care of breakfast and let you sleep in a bit."

"How sweet of you." Her hand fell from his stomach and she stretched her arm over her head. "I had a bit of a late night so sleeping in felt nice."

He swallowed and struggled not to let his mind go back to last night, or how they'd put a good dent in the box of condoms, before he slipped into his own bed in the wee hours of the morning. He gestured toward the cupboard. "You want to grab three plates? These won't take long."

Moving away from him she grabbed the plates and set the table. "What are your plans for the day?" She took a seat next to Ava.

Ava held her finger up. "Mommy, I don't need a bandage anymore."

"Look at that, it's just about healed." Rachel looked over her finger. "Just be careful with the wood, okay?"

Kyle poured the batter into the pan and grabbed Rachel a cup of coffee. He added a splash of milk and set it in front of her.

"Sleeping in, breakfast, and now coffee. I could get used to this." She gave him a smile.

Yeah, she wasn't the only one.

"I want to stop by to see Jack. I ordered in a new chain sprocket. My bike has been sitting so long I have a corroded link. After that, Ava and I are going to work on the tree house."

"Can we go to the pool too?" she asked.

He ruffled her hair. "Sure, squirt."

"Can we go see if Lindsay's mommy will take her so we can play?"

At the mention of Lindsay's mom Rachel tightened. "I'm sure Lindsay will like that," Kyle said.

She shot Kyle a glance. "And so will her mom."

Whoa, was that jealousy?

Kyle leaned against the counter and folded his arms. "Lindsay and her mom do seem to enjoy the pool," he said.

"Lindsay's mommy and her friends said they liked the new view. What's the new view, Mommy?"

Rachel nearly choked on her coffee. "Nothing for you to worry about." She tapped Ava's nose. "You make sure you wear sunscreen, okay?"

"Okay," she agreed.

"You too," she said to Kyle. "Or I'll have to coat you in aloe vera again."

A tremble moved through Kyle as he flipped the pancakes. Mother and daughter talked as he turned the burner up. As soon as the pancakes were done, he divided them up and sat at his usual spot.

*His usual spot.*

Shit he really was growing comfortable here. Really could

get used to this. But he was leaving soon, and while playing house was nice—damn nice—it would be behind him in a few short weeks.

They all chatted quietly as they ate, then Rachel glanced at the clock. "I'd better get going. Don't want to be late."

She reached for her plate, but Kyle stopped her, his hand closing over hers. "I got this."

"I can do the dishes," she said, her voice a little raspier than it was moments ago.

He brushed his thumb over her wrist, and she drew in a little shuddery breath. "I know you can, but I want to help out while I'm here."

"You're already doing so much."

But when it came to her it was never enough. "Go." He released her hand. "Get ready."

She took off upstairs as Kyle gathered the plates and put them in the sink. "Do you want to wash or dry, squirt?"

"Wash!"

Ava jumped from the chair and he dragged it over to the sink. She climbed on as he filled the basin with warm soapy water and gave her a rag. Ava giggled as she played with the suds, tossing them in the air and soaking her face.

Kyle laughed at her. "I take it you've never washed the dishes before."

"No, Mommy washes." She shook her hands, flicked the bubbles in all directions and soaked Kyle's shirt.

"Hands in the water, soldier," he commanded.

She giggled. "I'm not a soldier."

"Today you are." He reached over her and showed her how to wash the dishes. "Like this."

"This is fun," she said. He rinsed the plate and put it in the dish tray.

He gave her a salute. "You're on your own, soldier."

She laughed and ran the rag over the plate. Kyle reached

for the dish towel hanging from the stove and the sound of Rachel's indrawn breath had him turning. She stood in the doorway, the emotions in her eyes as she watched them tightened his throat.

He angled his head, taking in the stiffness in her body. "You okay?"

"Yeah, I just ah..." She waved her thumb over her shoulder. "Just heading out."

"Okay, we'll see you at dinner."

"Bye, Mommy."

Her heels clicked and she seemed completely out of sorts as she crossed the small room to give Ava a kiss. But Ava was so busy splashing water everywhere she barely spared her mother a glance.

Rachel made a face and backed up before Ava soaked her. "You be a good girl. Do what Kyle tells you."

"Don't worry, she's always good and she's in capable hands." He grimaced. "Well, most times."

Her hand brushed against his and her face smoothed out. "Always," she said. "I would never leave her with someone I didn't trust completely."

Shaken by the warm, needy look on her face and the way she ran her tongue over her bottom lip, Kyle inclined his head, a storm rolling through him. Christ, being around her and not being able to touch her unless they were behind closed doors was getting harder and harder.

As her soft hands lingered on his, raw hunger roared through him and overshadowed every rational thought. He leaned in to her and pressed his lips to hers. The sweetness of her mouth wrapped around his heart as everything about this situation flipped his world upside down.

With her back still to them, Ava squealed and he inched away to see her toss more bubbles in to the air. He brushed his thumb over Rachel's flushed cheek. "See you tonight," he whispered, and she nodded. He couldn't take his eyes off her as she left the room, her backside sashaying with each step.

He drew a quick breath to clear his head and turned to Ava. "Okay, squirt. Let's finish these up and go see Jack."

"I want to play," she protested, splashing her hands in the water and drenching the counter.

Kyle soaked up the water with his dish towel. "Okay, but did I tell you Jack has a big German Shepherd dog named Colby?"

Her eyes lit and her hands stilled. "Can I play with Colby?"

"Not if you stay here."

"I want to come."

He dabbed her cheeks with the cloth. "Okay. Let's get changed and then we can go."

With everything wet and slippery, he helped her from the chair and she darted toward the stairs. Kyle made quick work of the dishes, and after drying the counter and cupboards, he went to his room to get changed.

Twenty minutes later he pulled his truck in to the parking lot of Freedom Cycles and helped Ava from the cab. He held her hand in the lot and guided her inside the building. He glanced around, looking for Jack, but when he found the front counter empty, he stepped into the back workshop to find his friend bent over an Italian Aprilia motorcycle.

Kyle looked over the bike. "We don't see many of those around here."

Jack stood and wiped a cloth over his brow. "I was wondering when I was going to see your sorry..." He paused when he noticed a big-eyed Ava staring up at him. "Ah, never mind. You snuck your things out of here like a damn thief in the night."

"Sorry about that. I guess by now you heard I was staying

at Rachel's and taking care of Ava." He swung Ava's arm, and she smiled. "Ava, this is Jack."

"Hey, Ava."

"Hi." She twirled her finger around the pigtail she insisted he put in again this morning. He was going to have to get a lesson one of these days. "Do you have a dog?"

"You bet I do." Jack laughed. "Cute kid. She looks like you."

"She looks like her father," he said, and once again, a strange sensation gathered in his stomach.

"Would you like to meet Colby?" Jack asked. She nodded. "He's big, but he won't hurt you. You're not afraid of big dogs, are you?"

"Cuddles is big and she would never hurt me."

Jack exchanged a look with Kyle but didn't question him. Jack opened the back door, and a chain rattled before Colby came running at them.

"Hey, boy." Kyle went down on one knee and grabbed him before he knocked Ava over.

"Colby," she squealed and when Colby turned his attention to her and she started petting him, he stood and looked at the bike again.

He put his hand in his pockets. "What's the problem?"

"Damned if I know. I'm not an expert on these foreign models. It keeps shorting out and the only thing I can figure out is it's in the wiring."

Kyle dropped down and looked it over. As an explosives expert, wiring was his thing. He played with it for a few minutes, unplugging each module and resetting them. He pulled the throttle position censor, and when the bike started, he said, "Here's your problem. The throttle position censor isn't sending electrical signals. If you don't want to replace it, I can trace the wiring and find which one it is." He stood to find Jack staring at him. "What?"

Jack shook his head. "You know, you're a lot smarter than you look."

With Ava playing on the floor next to him, he mouthed the words "fuck off".

Jack laughed and wiped his hands on a rag. "Why don't you forget about the army and come work for me?"

Kyle cupped the back of his neck. "That's the second offer I've had this week."

The smile fell from Jack's face. Every one of his friends knew he didn't get along with his folks. "Your dad?"

He nodded. "Yeah. He still has that corner office waiting."

"You're considering it," Jacks said.

"What makes you say that?"

Jack shrugged. "I don't know. Gut feeling, I guess."

Kyle snorted, even though his friend was right. Well, technically Jack wasn't right. He wasn't really considering it. It was just something he'd always wanted. "Your gut's off this time, pal. I have no reason to stay."

Jack folded his arms, looked at Ava then back at Kyle. All seriousness gone from his face, he said, "You sure about that?"

Kyle's gaze traveled to Ava, who was giggling as Colby licked her face, and his gut clenched. She was so sweet, and he loved spending time with her. Then there was Rachel. He wanted to do for her, wanted to be there, but he couldn't just step into his brother's shoes. It was wrong. Right? Honest to fuck, he wasn't sure about anything anymore. He drove his hands into his pockets and swallowed past the lump in his throat. "So about that part for my bike. Did it come yet?" he asked, redirecting the conversation.

"I'll get it."

Jack rooted around on the shelves and Kyle walked in to the front storeroom. He hadn't noticed it earlier, but the second he spotted a kids' bike section he called Ava.

"Ava, come here."

She skipped into the showroom, Colby wagging his tail behind her. "What do you think of those?" He pointed to row of bikes near the window.

Her eyes went wide when she saw the pink, three-wheel electric motorcycle, and she clapped. She hurried over to it, and he scooped her up and set her on it.

"Made for a princess." He'd been trying to make her into a tomboy, but this bike had Ava written all over it. Honestly though, she could be a princess as long as he was around. He'd protect her, like he did her mother. It was when he was gone, that she'd need to learn to take care of herself. The thought of that actually turned his stomach upside down, the pancake he'd eaten earlier roiling in his gut. Every little girl needed a dad in her life.

*You don't have to go.*

Whoa, where the hell did that thought come from?

Jack came back with a box in his hand, and looked at the row of electric bikes. "Cute, aren't they?"

"When did you start carrying them?"

"Since Cole ordered one for his daughter." Jack grabbed a helmet, bent forward and put it on Ava. "Safety first," he said.

She nodded in agreement, her face squished in the helmet. "Uncle Kyle forgot to put sunscreen on me, and I got a splinter," she said, acting like the most worldly four-year-old in the universe.

Jack laughed and put his hand on Kyle's shoulder. "If she's this precocious right now, she's going to be one hell of a teen to raise. Good thing she has you to keep her on the straight and narrow."

He looked at his friend, his words hitting like a sucker punch. Ava was a smart, strong-willed girl, and Jack was right, she was going to be a hell of a teen. As a single mom, Rachel had her job cut out for her.

The door overhead jangled, and when a customer walked

in, Jack excused himself. "What do you think, Ava? Would you like to have this?" She squealed and clapped her hands. Colby nudged her, his tail wagging madly. "You do have a birthday coming up."

"Do we have to ask Mommy?"

He probably should, but Ava was his niece, dammit, and if he wanted to buy her a bike for her birthday, then he should be allowed. "Nope." He gestured to Jack and said, "We'll take it."

Rachel was going to kill him.

**10**

After whipping up a salad for Matt's upcoming afternoon barbeque, Rachel put the bowl in the fridge and poured herself a cup of coffee. She opened the back door and tightened her robe around her waist, enjoying her lazy Saturday morning.

She stepped onto the deck and sipped her hot brew as she watched Kyle and Ava work on the tree house. Well, Kyle was working while Ava drove around the backyard on her princess motorcycle. Her heart nearly exploded every time she saw the two together, the secret between them growing bigger, all consuming, threatening to rip her heart into a million pieces. Maybe she should have told him that first day and taken her chances that he wouldn't hate her. Sure she wanted him to grow to love them first, and not feel like he'd betrayed his brother, but now she had no idea how to tell him and the longer she waited the worse it was going to be.

"Mommy, look at me," Ava said and waved at her.

She forced a grin, her emotions a hot mess. She wasn't sure about her riding it at first. What if she crashed into something? Kyle assured her it was as safe as a bicycle and had bought her all the proper riding gear. It was an extravagant present, but Kyle swore it was to make up for all the birthdays he'd missed, and was going to miss in the future.

Her heart squeezed at that last thought. Even though they didn't talk about what would happen after Easter, and kept what was between them a secret, he'd been in her bed every night—making sweet, sweet love to her. The sex was anything but casual, even though he said it was all he had to offer. They connected on an even deeper level and experienced an intimacy unlike anything she'd ever experienced before. Something potent happened between them whether he wanted to believe it or not.

If he thought he was keeping his heart out of it, then he wouldn't be touching her with such gentle hands, or looking at her with tenderness backlighting those baby blues. If their lovemaking told her one thing, it was that he wanted her as much as she wanted him, and what they felt for each other went way beyond physical. He'd offered her his body, and for now that would have to do. But she didn't just want him in her bed, she wanted him in her life and could only hope by the time Easter rolled around, he'd realize he had a reason, two reasons to stay, and not hate her, or himself, when her secret came out.

Her mind took that moment to race back to when he'd torn her nightgown open, stripping it from her body like she was a gift he couldn't wait to get his hands on. Her body rippled in remembrance. She'd never seen that side of him, never seen him come undone like that before, but it was the start of something new between them. Whether he realized it or not, he was rebuilding his life.

She took another sip of her coffee and gazed at his bare torso over the rim of her cup. Her body quivered. His glance met hers, and his eyes darkened, like he could read all the naughty little things going on inside her head.

"How's it going?" she asked.

He lifted his hammer and pointed up. "Coming together. All that's left is the roof."

She glanced at her watch. "You've got about a half an hour then we have to go."

"I better quit now." He wiped his brow with his forearm. "I need to jump in the shower."

He dropped his hammer and gathered up the nails and tools. Ava drove toward him and he put his hand up to stop her. She slowed and he said, "Time to pack it in, squirt."

She frowned. "I don't want to. I want to play." She turned the throttle again and the bike started moving.

Rachel was about to intervene, but closed her mouth when Kyle said, "Okay, but Lexi is going to be there, remember? And you'll get to meet Charlotte and her little brother, Brandon. Murph would be also be very sad if you didn't go."

She eyed him. "Who's Murph?"

"Matt and Sky's dog." He could almost hear the wheels spinning in her brain. "You know who else is going to be there?"

"Colby?"

"Yup. Colby, Rex, Charlie, Stallone, and Nana. Nana is really, really old so she'll probably sleep." Her eyes grew wider and wider. "It's going to be so much fun. Lots of food, kids, and dogs for you to play with."

Ava jumped from the seat, and Kyle winked up at Rachel as he helped Ava take her helmet off. Her heart warmed. He had such a wonderful way with his little girl. He put the bike in the small shed as Ava came racing up the stairs to the house.

"Mommy, I want to wear my purple dress."

"Okay. It's in the laundry basket in my room."

Ava hurried through the house, her feet pounding on the stairs and Kyle climbed the ones next to her. He moved close, and her fingers tingled, not to mention another body part. He looked so rough and rugged, all she wanted to do was touch him—remove the rest of his clothes and take him to her bed and keep him forever.

He looked over her shoulder then in to the house. In a low voice he asked, "Where's Ava?"

"Upstairs looking for her dress."

His hand slid around her neck, and he stepped closer to her. Rachel grew breathless as he dipped his head. He was always so careful when Ava was around—he clearly didn't want to give the child the wrong idea—and never before had he gotten close when they were outside, where anyone could happen upon them. "Do you know how sexy you look in this robet?"

Her eyes widened and she laughed. Her robe was big and bulky and looked like a potato sack. She playfully whacked his chest and let her hand linger. "It's far from sexy, Kyle."

"Like hell it is," he growled. "And if you keep teasing me like this, walking around looking so hot all the time, you're going to pay."

A shiver moved through her. She remembered the way his hand had come down on her ass, and the way he rubbed her cheek to soothe the blissful sting he'd left behind. "You mean like you made me pay for touching you in the kitchen the other day."

"Exactly." Another growl sounded in his throat as his lips came closer. "Although I'm beginning to think you like it." He swiped his tongue over her bottom lip then moved in for a kiss. She stepped closer and pushed against him. Her hands went around his shoulders, and she let her nails scrape over his skin. A tremble moved through him. She loved the way he reacted to her touch.

"Mommy, I can't find it." Ava rushed toward them. They both quickly broke apart.

"Come on." She reached for Ava's hand. "I'll help you. I have to get dressed too."

Kyle followed them up the stairs and disappeared into the shower as she and Ava rooted through the basket for her favorite dress. Rachel pulled on a pair of shorts and T-shirt, then Ava came back into her room wanting her hair tied back.

Rachel pulled the chair out at her dressing table. "Hop on."

Ava climbed onto the chair and smiled at herself in the mirror.

Rachel reached for her comb, to brush out the tangles. Her glance wandered to the drawer where she kept her documents, and once again unease filled her. If he found out before she told him, it would surely kill him.

Kyle poked his head in. "All set?"

"I have to fix Ava's hair."

He laughed. "Better you than me."

She grinned at him. "Want a lesson?"

"Uh, not really but I guess I should learn." He crossed over to her and she slid the comb along the center of Ava's hair to part it. "Take this," she said, and he gathered up half her hair in his hand. "Now watch." She divided the hair into three sections and crossed them. "Like this." He followed her direction. "Pull it tighter, it won't hurt her."

He cringed. "I pulled it tight once and she said it hurt."

"Uncle Kyle isn't very good with braids," Ava said.

He laughed. "Then why do you keep asking me to do them?"

"I like them."

"Keep still, honey." Rachel looked at Kyle's braid and the way those big fingers of his were fumbling with his daughter's hair. He was so big and strong, all strength and power yet capable of such gentleness when he was with Ava. It nearly did her in.

She nudged him. "You got it."

"I know how to braid, I just never braided hair before, and she never sits still." He reached for the elastic on her nightstand and tied it off.

"Believe me, I know." Rachel leaned forward and kissed her daughter on the head. "All done."

She slid off the chair and ran out of the room. "Hurry. I want to see Lexi and Murph."

"I wish I could bottle that energy." Kyle shook his head.

"I know, right? Can you imagine what she's going to be like as a teen?" The smile fell from Kyle's face, and her stomach clenched. "What?"

"Oh, it was just that Jack said the same thing the other day."

"What?"

"Nothing really, but that reminds me. Dad wants us all to go to his place for Easter dinner."

Her eyes dropped to her feet, and she studied her polished toes. Most times she dropped Ava off for a visit. Rarely did she stay or share a meal. She wished Irene had more respect for her and realized that she hadn't married James for his money.

Kyle touched her chin, lifting it until their gazes met. "Hey, if you don't want to, we don't have to."

"You need to have Easter dinner with your folks and I know Ava would love it, but your mom and I—"

"I know." He cupped the side of her head and brushed his finger over her cheek.

"I wish it was different, Kyle. I really do. I've tried over the years."

"I know that too, and don't worry, if you do decide to go, I'll be by your side the whole time."

Her heart skipped a beat as her insides warmed. Somehow Kyle always made things better. "Okay. I'll go."

He nodded. "Dad also asked me to bring Ava to the cottage to go fishing, I was thinking the Saturday before Easter. Is that okay with you?"

She smiled. "Ava would love that."

He leaned in and planted a soft kiss on her lips. "Me too."

"Mommy," Ava called from downstairs.

Kyle stepped back, and waved his hand for Rachel to lead the way. "I guess we should go."

They met Ava at the foot of the stairs and Rachel grabbed her salad from the fridge. They fastened Ava into her car seat, and she handed Kyle the keys.

"Want to drive?"

Kyle slid into the driver's seat and Rachel climbed in the passenger side and set her salad on her lap. She looked out the window as he drove, feeling a bit uneasy. She hadn't seen the old group in years. What would they even talk about? How would they feel about her when they all learned the truth? At least Sara would be there.

Halfway to Matt's place, Kyle turned to her. "You okay?"

She smiled. How was it he was always so in tune with her emotions? "I just haven't seen them in so long. Since the funeral."

"I know." He went quiet for a long time, and she studied his hard profile. He turned, and his face softened when their eyes met. "Don't worry." His hand snaked out and slid across the seat to capture hers. He gave a reassuring squeeze. "I'll be there with you. If you're uncomfortable we'll leave. But I know it's going to be fine. They're going to love seeing you and you'll all fall back into an easy friendship. You'll see."

"Okay," she said. Kyle always made her feel better, but what if they could tell something was going on between them.

"Kyle?"

"Yeah."

She darted a glance into the back seat to find Ava bouncing in her car seat as she played with her doll. She lowered her voice. "What if they can tell?" Other than his brother, Kyle didn't much care what other people thought, but she did. She loved Kyle and didn't want anyone to think badly of her—or him—because of the situation.

"No one knows anything," he assured her.

Her stomach was in knots by the time they reached Matt's place. With the driveway full of cars, he parked on the street. Voices and laughter could be heard coming from the backyard. Kyle helped Ava from the backseat and Rachel was about to grab her hand when her daughter reached up and took Kyle's like it was the most natural thing in the world for her to do.

"Hurry, Uncle Kyle," she said, dragging him up the drive-way. Rachel watched them go, the word uncle ringing hollowly in her ears, and twisting her stomach. They followed the path around the back of the house. Before they reached the yard, Matt came around the side of the house to meet them.

"I thought I heard voices" He gave Kyle a hug, then focused on Rachel. A huge smile spread across his handsome face, and Rachel relaxed. "I'm so glad you came. We were all hoping you would." He angled his head to see Ava. She stared up at him, and he went down on one knee. "Hi, Ava, I'm Matt."

"Hi. Do you have a dog?"

Everyone laughed.

"She has a fixation," Kyle said.

"So I heard. Yes, I have a dog, and Lexi has been asking for you. Want to go find her?"

She nodded and he stood back up. "Here, let me take that." He reached for the salad bowl and then they all followed him along the gravel path leading to the back yard. Kyle put his hand on her back and splayed his fingers. His touch felt good, reassuring. They turned the corner and Rachel glanced around to see all her old friends sitting around in lawn chairs, talking and laughing.

Her best friend, Sara, was the first to jump up and give her a hug, followed by Gemma, Tallulah, Sky, Jenny, and Madison. Kyle stayed close to her side as she was introduced to Emery, who was Luke's wife, and Kat, Tallulah's best friend who'd moved here from Louisiana and worked at the hospital. After the introductions, the guys took turns hugging her. Most of the unease inside ebbed as they welcomed her back into the circle. Honestly, it felt good to be surrounded by her friends, to hang out with other adults for a change, but will they be so welcoming when Ava's paternity is revealed? Everyone said hello to Ava as dogs barked in the big back yard. She looked over to see the kids playing catch with the dogs. Ava tugged on her hand. "Mommy, can I go play?"

"Of course."

Ava took off to play with Lexi, Charlotte, and Brandon, and about five rambunctious dogs and one who just wanted to sleep in the sun. Must be Nana.

"Matt, grab Rachel a chair," Sky called out as she poured potato chips into a bowl.

"I got it." Kyle grabbed two folded lawn chairs, opened them and set them side-by-side.

Rachel lowered herself into it, and Kyle dropped down next to her. They exchanged a long look, Kyle checking to make sure she was comfortable. She loved how sensitive he was to her needs, how he made her feel warm inside and out. When she gave him a smile, he nodded in understanding and relaxed back into his seat.

Matt reached into a cooler. "Kyle," he called out and

tossed him a bottle of beer. He pulled another one out. "How about you, Rachel?"

Sky rolled her eyes at Matt and rubbed his back. As Rachel saw the two of them together she smiled. It was clear how much they loved each other. After all the years they'd been best friends, how did they finally end up together? It saddened her to think she didn't know, that she'd lost touch with everyone after James had died, and had buried herself in her work and raising her daughter.

"How about a glass of wine?" Sky asked her.

"Sounds perfect."

Sky poured her a glass of merlot and refilled everyone else's. She grabbed a bottle of water and sat down.

"I hope everyone is hungry." Matt lifted the lid on the barbeque to flip the burgers and hotdogs.

Rachel glanced at all the condiments on the table, and shook her head when she saw the big jar of peanut butter. Matt and his peanut butter. Honest to God, the guy was too funny.

"Wait," Gemma said, her glass stilling inches from her lips as she zeroed in on Sky. "Why aren't you drinking?"

Sky grinned, her smile stretching a mile wide. "Well..." she said. "We're not just celebrating Matt passing the MCATs and getting in to medical school."

"Ohmigod," Tallulah squealed and jumped from her chair. "You're pregnant."

"I know we're supposed to wait three months to announce, but I couldn't keep it from you guys any longer."

Everyone hugged again and the guys all patted Matt on the back.

"Guess the boys were working after all," Caleb said, and the guys all laughed at the comment. He clinked bottles with Kyle. "Like I told you, there's something in the water."

Sky swatted him. "You wait, Caleb. One of these days

someone is going to turn your world inside out and you'll want a brood of kids with her."

"Until then, I'm sticking with my beer." He grinned at Kyle. "You with me, buddy?"

Kyle laughed and took a long pull from his bottle, and Rachel didn't miss the way his glance flickered to her, uncertainly backlighting his eyes when he said, "I'm with you."

Sky waved her finger at him. "Your day will come too, Kyle. You just watch and see."

He gave a slow shake of his head, stretched his legs out and crossed them at the ankles. "Not gonna happen."

"I call bullshit," Jack said.

"Me too," Madison piped in. She pointed to Ava, who was laughing and playing with the kids and dogs. "That little girl has you wrapped around her finger."

"Come on, she's my niece, and I want to spoil her while I'm here."

"Hey, am I late?" a male voice asked.

Rachel turned to see a boy around fifteen or sixteen come around the corner. She looked him over but had no idea who he was.

"Trent," Luke said, jumping up. He slung his arm around Trent's shoulder, and the boy beamed up at him. "Not late at all. Just in time."

"I was late getting away," Trent explained.

Luke nodded. "I think you know everyone here but Rachel and Kyle." They both shook his hand and Luke explained. "Trent volunteers at Sheffield Community Center on Saturdays. He also works with Emery at the store a few evenings a week."

"Don't forget the drive-in." He shoved his hands into his pockets. "I work there Saturday nights."

"I didn't think that place would still be open," Kyle said.

"It was run-down when we were kids." He shot Rachel a glance. "Wasn't it?"

She nodded in agreement. Even though it had been one of her favorite hang out places, James rarely went with them. He hated being confined in the car, but she and Kyle loved it. They'd gorged on popcorn and pop and spent more time talking than they did watching the movie anyway. She grinned. How many times had she convinced him to watch a chic flick with her?

Trent laughed. "The place is old. But I like it. I get to watch free movies, and sometimes I can bring my brother. My friend, Allison, works in the canteen and she always gives him free licorice."

"Allison, huh," Luke said. "Is she cute?"

Trent's cheeks turned red, and he elbowed Luke in the gut playfully. "None of your business." Luke let out a loud, exaggerated *oomph* and grabbed Trent a chair as the boy reached into the bowl for a handful of potato chips. Rachel wasn't sure how the two knew each other, but it was clear from the way Trent looked at Luke that he thought of him as a father figure. Much like the way Ava looked at Kyle. Except Kyle really was her father.

"Mommy," Ava called out.

Kyle angled his head, and his face softened when he saw Ava coming his way, carrying Brandon, who was about two. She struggled to walk, and was undoubtedly squeezing the life out of the poor boy. "Mommy, Charlotte says Brandon can be my baby brother too."

Charlotte came skipping up behind them. "We're gonna share," she said. "And Ava said I could play in her tree house."

Ava set Brandon down and patted him on the head.

"Looks like the kids are hitting it off," Gemma said. "Maybe Ava would like to come over for a sleepover sometime." Her glance went from Rachel, to Kyle, then back to

Rachel again. "Give the adults a night off," she paused, gave her a wink and added, "You know, to do adult things."

Rachel cringed against the wave of heat moving up her neck. Oh, God, did Gemma know? She looked around at the group of women, who were grinning at her like they were all in on her secret—at least one of them. Of course they knew. From the energy between her and Kyle, to the way they touched, looked at each other and stayed close spoke volumes. No doubt they could feel the connection between them every bit as much as she felt it between the newly engaged Matt and Sky. But they were smiling, not judging. Her heart swelled even more, and tears pricked her eyes. Sara was right. These people were her friends and had her back, no matter what. Here, in the circle of their friends, she and Kyle were surrounded by love and acceptance. And maybe, just maybe they wouldn't hate her, or Kyle, when the other truth came out.

"I...uh..." she began.

"How about next Saturday night? We'd love to take Ava, wouldn't we, Cole?"

"Sure," Cole said, only half listening as he talked about some football game with Brad.

Matt turned the burners off on the barbecue. "Food's ready."

Kyle scooped Ava up. "Hey, squirt, you want something to eat?" Rachel's heart squeezed so hard it hurt to breathe as she watched Kyle with Ava. In her eyes they created the perfect little family. But what about Kyle? Did he really not want kids? If that was the case, then what would he do when he found out the little girl in his arms was his?

11

It was strange how nervous Rachel felt. She fixed her hair in the mirror for the hundredth time, and reapplied her lipstick because she kept eating it off with her teeth. Perhaps her anxiety stemmed from Ava's first sleepover, or perhaps it had more to do with the fact that she and Kyle had the entire night together, alone, and it would be a good night for them to talk.

The shower turned off and Kyle's footsteps sounded on the floor as he walked down the hall to his room. She could only imagine he was wrapped in a towel, his gorgeous body on display. If she hurried maybe she could get a peek at him before he dressed. It wasn't like she had to worry about Ava catching them. Gemma had insisted Ava have dinner with the family, so they'd dropped her off earlier that day.

She pushed away from her dressing table and smoothed her hand over her summery dress. She wasn't sure where they were going. Kyle said it was a surprise, so she had no idea if she was overdressed or underdressed. Her door creaked as she opened it.

"Kyle," she called out as she walked the few steps to his door.

"Yeah."

"Am I dressed okay?"

His door opened and when she found him standing there in a towel, her mouth watered. His gaze dropped to her dress and his nostrils flared. "Jesus, you are so hot."

In a move that was becoming very familiar to her, he gripped the back of her neck and pulled her to him. He smelled like soap and ocean and something uniquely Kyle. She pressed against him and could feel his growing erection against her stomach. His warm lips fell over hers and he kissed her. Softly at first, his lips gilding gently over hers, but when she moaned and slipped her hand between their bodies to touch his cock, he deepened the kiss. His tongue slid into her mouth and hungrily slashed against hers. The air grew thick and hot between them.

Her body turned warm as his cock throbbed in her hands, and in that moment there was nothing she wanted more than to take him into her mouth and taste him, pleasure him. He seemed to have a thing about her pleasing him orally, however. She wasn't sure what it was, and after that first time, he never let her do it again. It was time to change that. Her finger went to the knot in the towel, but he jerked back, his breathing labored.

"If we don't stop this, we'll never get out of here." He raked a shaky hand through his hair and moved farther away, severing the intimacy between them.

Refusing to let him retreat, she stepped back in to him and put her hand on his chest. He briefly closed his eyes, the way he always did when she touched him. "Is there somewhere we have to be?"

He swallowed. Hard. "Yeah."

Her finger trailed over his hard muscles, dipping into the

grooves and ridges of his six-pack. His whole body quaked and she smiled. She loved when he shivered like that. "How much time do we have?"

He looked at the clock, heat and need dancing in his eyes. "Half hour," he croaked out.

Poor guy, he was in bad shape. She grinned and released his towel, damn well determined to do something about the state he was in. It fell to the floor and she sank to her knees right along with it "Then maybe there is time for this."

"Rach. Jesus, Rach." He gripped her hair and pushed her away. "You don't have to do that. Not for me."

She wrapped her hands around his cock, and stole a peek at him. "Who says it's for you?" she challenged.

"Rach," he moaned sounding like he was in pure agony. "Come on. I know you don't like that."

She blinked up at him and met with eyes that always turned soft when looking at her. Her gaze moved over his face, assessing him. Why the heck did he think she didn't like taking him into her mouth? Whatever gave him that idea?

She lifted her chin in defiance. "Looks like there is one thing you don't know about me after all."

"Rach—" he began, but she cut him off.

"Kyle, there isn't a single part of your body that I don't want to kiss..." She leaned forward and swiped her tongue over his crown. His cock thickened, stretching toward her lips. "Or lick." She lifted her head and their eyes met and locked. "I told you I wanted you. All of you."

He sucked in a quick breath. "You know I can't...oh, fuck." His protest died on his lips and was replaced by a moan when she drew him in and sucked hard. They both wanted this and there was nothing he could do or say to stop her. His hands curled through her hair, but this time it wasn't to push her away; it was to hold her close.

She whimpered and drew him in as much as she could. He

hit the back of her throat, and when she choked a little, he cursed and tried to pull out. Instead of letting him, she cupped his balls and massaged lightly as she took him to the back of her throat again.

"Christ, that's so fucking good."

Her body quivered, reveling in the hard length of him, the salty taste of his skin. She worked her tongue over his length, and ribbons of need zinged through her veins. He rocked his hips and thrust against her mouth. She swirled her tongue around his crown, then relaxed her throat to take him in even deeper. She fondled his balls gently and used her other hand in tandem with her mouth, sliding it up and down his cock until his heavy breathing echoed in the room. He might not want her to do this, but he liked it. A lot. She pulled out and pressed her tongue against the sensitive underside of his crown until a strangled noise crawled out of his throat.

His cock pulsed and her body reacted. Her breasts grew heavy, and her nipples tingled, aching to be suckled. But she was taking too much joy in pleasuring him to stop and answer the demands of her body. With an empty house until morning, there would be time for that later.

"Oh fuck," he cried out, and tried to pull her away, but she stayed between his legs, wanting him to let go in her mouth. He pulsed against her throat as his veins filled with heated blood. "Rach," he croaked out. "I need you to stop."

Ignoring his plea, she worked him harder, and his fingers tightened in her hair until he was pulling it, hard. Pain and pleasure mingled into one as she licked and sucked until he was past the point of no return.

"Oh, Christ." What could only be classified as a primal, animalistic growl rumbled in his throat as he filled her mouth with his release. She drank him in, swallowing every last drop.

Other than his raspy sounds catching in his throat, they both remained quiet. She stayed nestled between his legs, and he gently stroked her hair as they both struggled to breathe. Silence reined for a minute, then his hands left her hair and moved to her shoulders. A quick tug and she was on her feet. His eyes moved over her face, warm and tender as he studied her. Silence fell over them again as he placed his palm on her cheek, his thumb stroking gently.

He started to back her up toward the bed, but she shook her head to stop him. "No, Kyle. We don't have time."

He frowned and shook his head. "That's not my style, Rach."

She put her hand on his chest and enjoyed the feel of his strong heart beneath her palm. His muscles quivered and jumped beneath her fingers. "I know, and it's one of the many things I love about you."

As soon as the word *love* left her lips, he stiffened. The truth was she wanted to talk to him, but as she looked at him now, she didn't want to let anything come between them and ruin this special night together. There was always tomorrow... She put on a smile, glanced at the clock and tried to lighten the mood. "Well, maybe we do have time. That didn't take too long."

"Hey," he shot back laughing. "Play nice." He looked at the clock, and a sheepish grin tugged at the corners of his mouth. "Uh, okay, yeah, maybe you're right. But what the hell do you expect?" He fisted his hair. "Jesus, Rachel, that was pretty damn incredible."

Pride swelled inside her. "You like my mouth on you."

He gave her a look that suggested she was crazy. "You think?"

She went up on her toes and planted a soft kiss on his lips. "Then let me do it more often."

He shrugged. "I guess. I mean, if you insist."

Loving this playful side of him, a side she hadn't seen in so long, she ran her hands over her clothes to smooth them. "Seriously though, we should get going."

He grabbed her by the waist. "Fine. But I'm not done with you. Not by a long shot."

"That's what I was hoping for."

Kyle hurried into his clothes and she stood in the doorway for a second, watching the play of his muscles. Her sex clenched. While she would like nothing better than for him to have his way with her, there'd be time for that later. He seemed excited about taking her some place and she was anxious to find out where. She wiped her brow to find it damp and dashed into the bathroom to tidy herself up.

By the time she finished she found Kyle in the hall putting his watch on as he waited for her. "All set?" She nodded and he put his hand on her back to guide her to the stairs. She grabbed her purse and darkness was just beginning to fall over the city as she walked toward her car, but Kyle turned her.

"Let's take the truck." He opened the door and she slid in.

"Where are we going?"

"You'll see."

She eyed him. Why was he being so vague? He was clearly up to something. They drove to the outskirts of the city and when he pulled off and down a long road, she sat up straighter, taking in the big outdoor screen.

"You're kidding me."

He laughed. "Nope."

"Kyle, I haven't been here in so long." She laughed and shook her head. "Since we were teens."

"I know. You need to get out more."

"That's one of the things Sara said to me too."

"One of the things?"

"Yeah." She wasn't about to tell him all the other things, like seducing him into staying. He pulled up to the ticket booth and Trent greeted them, a grin on his face like he was up to something.

"What's playing?" she asked.

He exchanged a look with Kyle. "It's oldies night."

"Oldies night?" she laughed. Okay, to him they probably did seem old.

Kyle paid the entrance fee and drove through the near-empty parking lot. "I guess a lot of teens don't come out on oldies night." He parked and unhooked his seat belt. "I'll be right back."

She watched him until he disappeared inside the concession stand. A bubble of excitement welled up inside her to be back at one of their favorite hangout spots. Of course back then while the teens were making out, she and Kyle just talked about their plans, their futures. Never once had he mentioned joining the army. Which was why it had probably thrown her for such a loop when he'd up and left so quickly.

Kyle returned with a big box of popcorn and two drinks. She rolled her window down and he passed them through. She took a sip and laughed. Root beer. How long had it been since she drank root beer? Honest to God, it took her right back in time.

Kyle slid in beside her. "Right on time," he said as the opening advertisements began. He adjusted the old speaker on his window but no sound came. He rolled his window down, popped open the speaker and fiddled with the wires.

"Let's move to another spot."

"Do you have no faith in me?" he teased as he put the speaker back together again. A second later sound filled the cab of the truck.

She laughed. "You're a man of many talents, Kyle."

She munched her popcorn and thought about that. Kyle was smart but for as long as she had known him he played down his abilities. Just then the movie came on and she nearly choked on her popcorn.

*When Strangers Met* flashed on the screen.

"Oh. My. God." She blinked. "How did you...?"

He grinned. "I have connections."

"I can't believe you did this." She eyed him. "I thought you hated this movie."

The smile fell from his face, and something deeper, more serious flashed in his eyes. His voice was low when he said, "But you don't."

A lump gathered in her throat. He was the toughest guy she knew, yet so sweet and kind when it came to her and Ava.

She took a drink of her soda and placed it on the dashboard beside his. She put her popcorn on the floor and slid across the cab. A shaky palm went to his cheek and she placed a soft kiss on his mouth. He kissed her back with heat and passion. There was so much more to this man than anyone knew.

He cupped her head and inched back. Blue eyes stared at her for a long time, then he pressed a kiss to her forehead and turned toward the screen. They watched for a little while, but her mind was too preoccupied with other things to pay attention.

"Kyle."

"Yeah," he answered his fingers playing in her hair as he stared at the screen.

She shifted to face him. "Why did you join the army? Especially when your father wanted you to join his firm?"

His jaw clenched, then he shrugged easily. "Dad and I didn't get along and I wasn't as smart as James."

*He wasn't as smart as James?* That was bullshit and they both knew it.

"You're one of the hardest working guys I know, so why did you give up in school, and sports?"

He looked away, his shoulders stiffening. "I didn't enjoy those things anymore and I left because I had no reason to stay in Austin."

She touched his face, turning him back to her. "You had me," she said softly.

"No." His voice was rough, hurting. "I didn't."

The pain and hurt in his eyes cut deep into her soul. She swallowed, her heart aching for him. Oh. My. God. They'd always been close, but she never knew how much he actually cared for her back then. Or how much her engagement to James had slayed him, or left him feeling alone and lost.

"Kyle," she whispered. "You have me now." Never wanting them to be apart again, she lifted her chin and placed her lips over his, determined to prove they were right together and he needed to stop running.

His lips were stiff at first, but when she slid her tongue along the seam and teased them open he put his hand around her head and growled. He angled his head, deepening the kiss until she was left breathless. She moaned, and he nudged her until she fell back on the seat.

"Is this why you wanted to bring the truck?" she teased, trying to lighten the mood. "More room to maneuver during a make-out session?"

"Something like that," he said, the harshness in his voice giving way to softness. His mouth left her neck to go to her breasts. He kissed her nipples through her dress and they hardened from the heat of his mouth.

He ran his palm along her thigh, going higher and higher. The roughness of his hand glorious against her skin. His fingers found her panties, and he pushed the scrap of material to the side. The second his finger touched her clit, her hips came off the seat. Breathing became harder and in no time at all they'd steamed up the windows. Good thing too. She was an adult and didn't want to get caught making out with Kyle in the cab of a truck at the drive-in.

He dipped a finger inside her, and she greedily ripped at his shirt, needing her hands on his body. He shifted and his cock pressed against her leg as he put another finger inside her and stroked her clit with his thumb.

A moan ripped from her throat, her hands skimming over his strong back as he touched her intimately. He pressed against her. She could feel his desires, needs, and knew they matched her own. Sexual heat arced between them as he brought her higher and higher, his deft fingers swirling inside her, his thumb applying the perfect amount of pressure to her clit.

She clawed at his back, her breath coming quicker as he worked her body, taking her higher and higher, in the way only he knew how.

"I'm right there," she cried out, but suspected he already knew. He changed the pace and pressure and a second later a violent quake moved through her. The love inside her heart rushed over her like a windstorm as her body let go. He kept his fingers insider her until her body stopped trembling.

He inched back and all she could do was stare as he unzipped his pants and pushed them down just enough to release his cock. He stroked it, and she ran her thumb over his swollen crown.

His eyes briefly shut. "Fuck, that feels good."

"Please tell me you have a condom," she whispered. He pulled one from the front pocket of his jeans and she chuckled breathlessly. "You really did have this planned."

His grin was boyish and seductive at the same time. "I just like to be prepared," he said, admitting to nothing.

He ripped into the condom and she took it from him to roll it down. He shook his head like he was in pure agony. Once she finished, he slipped his hands under her dress. Her body burned as his fingers raced up her thighs to the band on her panties. A quick tug and he dragged the slip of material from her hips. Without his eyes ever leaving hers, she lifted for him and he pulled her panties away, tucking them in his back pocket.

Being with Kyle like this, most of their clothes still on as they made out in a vehicle, felt so naughty, so exciting. She'd be lying if she said she'd never thought about this exact situation back in the day, when they were all in high school and she and Kyle would hang out in his car. While the two had been incredibly close, he always pulled back when it came to her, never offering her anything more than friendship—before that day at the bluff.

But what they were doing now went so much deeper than fun, hurried, high school sex in the cab of a truck. She was pretty sure he knew that every bit as much as she did.

Kyle fell over her and her sex fluttered in anticipation. "Open for me, babe," he commanded in a soft voice.

She widened her legs, offering him her body and her heart.

Warm lips found hers and he captured her mouth in a kiss full of passion and possession as he teased his cock between her legs. He brushed his crown over her clit, drawing out the seduction. She wiggled, urging him to hurry, to stop torturing her.

"Please," she begged. "I need you inside me."

"I know, babe, I know." His tongue brushed over hers and he growled into her mouth. "I can't ever seem to get enough of you either."

She wrapped her legs around him, forcing him in. "Just take, Kyle. Take everything you need."

Her words triggered a reaction in him. His hips jerked and he drove impossibly deeper, like he was seeking more than just release. Her muscles tightened around him and squeezed as he pumped, slow at first but picking up momentum as she met and welcomed each beautiful thrust.

"Rach," he murmured and buried his face in her neck. "Jesus, Rach..."

The need in his voice aroused her even more. She moved against him, grinding her clit against his pelvis each time he came down over her body. He raked shaky hands through her hair and fisted her curls. His breath was hot on her neck as he panted, like he was struggling to bring in air.

"That's so good," she said, her voice a low, strained whisper as she reveled in his hard length, his thick girth. She took a quick breath as her body let go, tumbling into orgasm once again. Kyle growled and stilled inside her, his cock throbbing as he joined her in release.

As they climaxed together, each sweet spasm brought them closer and closer together, creating an even deeper bond between them. Contentment raced through her and he held her tighter. Still joined as one, he collapsed on top of her, and their hearts and souls merged. She melted against him, and as she absorbed his heat, she felt so cherished, so loved in his arms. Everything about them felt right and all she could pray for was that nothing, not even her secret, could tear them apart now.

$$12$$

"That's yucky, Uncle Kyle," Ava said as Kyle threaded her worm through the hook. Ava squirmed on the dock beside him, making a face that showcased complete disgust, as Kyle's father laughed at her antics.

Once Kyle finished with the worm, he showed Ava how to hold the rod and cast it into the water. "Now, you watch that bobber. When it moves, or dips under the water, you take this handle and start turning it. That will bring in the fish."

She nodded, her disgust replaced by intense concentration as she very carefully stared at the bobber in anticipation. How long would that last? With the kind of energy she had, if she didn't catch something in seconds, she'd be bored out of her mind. After situating Ava, Kyle cast his own rod, and relaxed on the dock, enjoying the warm morning sun beating down on them.

His father adjusted his hat, looked out over the placid water and said, "I'm glad you came and brought Ava by. Your mother and I love spending time with her."

"She's a great kid." He stole a glance at the sweet little girl beside him.

"We don't see Rachel enough."

His head jerked to the right to find his father watching him with deep concern in his eyes. Kyle stiffened and considered how to respond. He was pretty sure no matter what came out of his mouth, it would end in a fight, so instead he just remained quiet.

"Will you all be coming to Easter dinner tomorrow night at the house?" his father asked, breaking the sudden uncomfortable quiet.

"Yeah, what time?"

"Six."

Ava huffed beside him, and kicked her legs out. "It's not doing anything. Why isn't it doing anything?"

Kyle ruffled her hair. "Give it time, squirt."

The minutes passed slowly. For Kyle he enjoyed the relaxed pace. Ava on the other hand, was growing antsier by the minute. A boat went by and they all waved. Ava's eyes lit up.

She blinked up at him. "Can we go out on Grandpa's boat?"

"Maybe later." Kyle said. "How about for now you go see if Grandma needs any help in the kitchen? I bet if you ask really nice, she might bake cookies with you."

She crinkled her nose. "But I want to catch a fish."

Kyle took the rod from her. "I'll tell you what. If your bobber moves I'll call you, okay?"

Ava jumped to her feet and, squeezed his face in typical Ava fashion. "Okay."

She took off running, and Kyle laughed. "She's really something, isn't she?"

"She is. You were right. Rachel is doing a good job with her."

Kyle's gaze darted back to his father again. The man had seriously mellowed over the years. "Yeah, she is," he agreed quietly.

"So are you," his father added.

A noise came out of Kyle's throat. A half laugh, half snort. Had his father just complimented him? Maybe they'd been out in the sun longer than he thought.

His father looked up at the cottage then back at Kyle. "It's easy to see that you two have grown pretty close over the last week."

"Yeah, we have. I'm going to miss her."

"And Rachel?" his father said. At the mention of her name, Kyle felt a possessive tug on his emotions. "Are you going to miss her too?"

A wave of unease moved through him. Where the hell was his father going with this? "What are you getting at?" He stiffened, going on the defensive.

His father cleared his throat and Kyle knew things were about to turn serious. "Kyle," he began, his voice soft, a bit cautious. "You love her."

*What the hell?* Those were the last three words he expected to spill from his father's mouth.

"I've always known, son. Everyone has."

He gave a hard shake of his head, a tightness building in his chest. "You're wrong. She was James's girl," he countered. "She was never mine."

"Only because James acted first." Reg's bobber disappeared under the water, and he gave a quick tug on his rod and reeled in his line, the clicking sound filling the moment of silence. The fish fought back, and before Reg could get it close enough, it freed itself and got away. He reached into the bucket and grabbed another worm. "You've always given up everything for him, Kyle."

Kyle toyed with the reel handle, his breath shakier than it

was moments ago. "What are you talking about?"

In spite of the serious conversation they found themselves in, his father laughed and nudged him with his shoulder. "I'm not the idiot you think I am."

"I never said you were an idiot." He glanced at his father, and they exchanged a long look. There was an understanding in the man's eyes Kyle had never seen before.

"And you, my son, are a hell of a lot smarter than you let on." Reg cast his rod again, went quiet for a long time. "I miss James." The sadness in his voice cut Kyle to the core. Reg pulled in a breath and let it out slowly. "I miss him so goddamn much. He was a good boy, with a bright future. It's not right that it was snatched away so suddenly." Reg put his hand on Kyle's shoulder and closed his fingers, holding Kyle tight, tighter than he ever had before. "I'm just glad you and Ava didn't inherit the condition."

Kyle's gut clenched and tears pricked his eyes. He pinched the bridge of his nose to suppress the flow and turned, struggling to contain his emotions. He strove to keep it together, but talking about James, and the life he lost, was hard, damn hard. He was the best older brother a guy could ask for and was everything to Kyle. His death had ripped his heart in two.

With his hand still on Kyle's shoulder, his father said, "It's time for you to take what you want, Kyle."

Kyle swallowed against the tightness in his throat and worked to keep his voice steady when he spoke. "What are you talking about?"

"It's time for you and Rachel to live the lives you were meant to live."

His father's words caught him off guard and he nearly swallowed his tongue. "What?"

"I know James would have wanted both Rachel and Ava to be loved and taken care of."

He shook his head hard. "But—"

"He'd want the one person he loved most, the one person who loved Rachel as much as he did to be there when he couldn't be," he said, his voice trembling with emotion.

Kyle's hands clenched around his rod hard enough to break it as his heart thundered in his ears. "I'm not about to step into his shoes and take over, if that's what you're getting at. It's wrong."

"You're not stepping into his shoes. You're forging your own path." He laughed and shook his head. "Lord knows you're good at doing things your way."

He took in the sadness on his father's face. His rebellion had been hard on them. "I'm sorry, Dad. I was a shitty son."

"Never be sorry. Everything you did, you did for James. I know that now, Kyle. You're the best brother—best man—I know." A garbled sound caught in his father's throat when he added, "I'm sorry I never told you that before."

His father's praise pulled the tears from his eyes. Kyle planted one elbow on his leg, and rested his forehead on it as he tried to choke them back. His efforts proved futile. They both went quiet for a long time, each trying to deal with their feelings the only way they knew how.

"Maybe it's time to do something just for you. Start thinking about what you want. It's easy to see how Rachel feels about you and that little girl needs a daddy."

He sat there trying to wrap his brain around what his father was telling him when he heard Ava.

"Uncle Kyle?"

Kyle sniffed, wiped his face and straightened at the sound of Ava's voice. "Hey, squirt. I didn't even hear you."

"What's wrong?" Her big eyes moved over his face in worry as she reached out and twirled her fingers in his hair.

"Nothing." It was a lie. Everything was wrong. He was in love with Rachel, as well as the sweet little girl in front of him. His own father was telling him to go after what he wanted, yet in three days he was scheduled to ship out. "What's up?"

Her brow knit together. "Are you going to be my daddy?"

"Sweetheart." His heart went in to his throat as he worried about how much she'd overheard. "That's not what we were saying at all." He grabbed her rod and held it out, desperate to distract her. "Did you want to fish again?"

She shook her head. "Grandma says it's time for lunch."

He reeled in his line, set it on the dock and jumped to his feet. Ava grabbed his hand and his heart squeezed. How could he ever walk away from her? But how could he stay without feeling like he'd betrayed his brother—again?

*Maybe it's time to do something just for you. Something you want.*

He walked with Ava up to the house, his father moving slowly behind them. The rest of the day passed in a blur and as evening approached, he packed Ava into the truck and drove them home.

He glanced up to see Rachel standing at the front door waiting for them. Dressed in a pair of jeans and T-shirt, her arms were folded across her chest as she leaned against the doorjamb. Looking sweet, sexy, and happy for the first time in a long time, she smiled at them. His heart turned inside out.

He wanted this. He wanted this so fucking bad. They hurried up the stairs to meet her, and after she kissed her daughter, Ava rushed to the bathroom to wash up for dinner. Kyle pulled Rachel in to his arms and planted a hungry kiss on her mouth.

She inched back, her eyes wide. "What was that for?"

He rolled his shoulder. "No reason, other than I wanted to."

She angled her head. "Is everything okay? You didn't get in a fight with your parents did you?"

"No, actually Dad and I had a good talk." He let out a

slow breath, the load on his shoulders lightening a little. "First time in a long time."

She smiled and touched his face. "I'm so glad to hear that, Kyle. I'd do anything to have one more minute with my dad. I'm happy to see you mending fences with him. It's important. Family is important."

"You're right. Family is important."

She looked him over for another second, her eyes narrowing. Then she glanced down at his empty hands and teasingly said, "I thought we were having fish for dinner."

He held his palms out, about nine inches apart. "I caught one this big, but it got away."

"Right." She laughed. "Come on, I made dinner."

He followed her down the hall and dashed into the bathroom behind Ava to wash up.

They all sat around the table like a family, Ava talked about worms and fishing and baking with Grandma as they ate. Once dinner was over, he did the dishes while Rachel gave Ava a bath, read her a book, and tucked her in.

"You meeting the guys tonight?" she asked, coming back in to the kitchen carrying a big brown grocery bag.

Kyle wrapped the dish towel around the oven handle "No, I thought I'd stay in. Have a beer. Watch a movie." He stepped closer and tucked her hair behind her ears. "Then you know, let you tear my clothes off and have your way with me."

She laughed. "Sounds good, but first I have some chocolate eggs to hide. Want to help?"

He smiled. He had such fond memories of hunting for Easter eggs with James.

He peeked in to the bag. "Anything for me in there?"

"Don't worry, you'll get something sweet later."

"Jesus," he said, his cock thickening as she teased him. He grabbed the bag. "Let's hurry then."

He helped Rachel hide the eggs, then laid out a chocolate bunny, a new doll, and a skipping rope on the table.

"What, no train?"

She laughed and lightly punched him in the gut. "No train."

He grabbed her and pulled her into his arms. She rested her head against him and as they stood together looking over Ava's Easter presents, his heart thudded. This all felt so right.

"Rach," he whispered, everything in him screaming possession.

"Yeah."

He glanced at the woman smiling up at him, and thought about the little girl in the bed upstairs. He wanted this. All of this.

"I'm ready for something sweet now."

———

Ava hopped around on the floor in front of the sofa, her energy at an all new high after indulging in too many Easter treats earlier that day. Now here they were, at Irene and Reg's for a family dinner, Ava chatting their ears off.

"And after the Easter egg hunt," she continued, "I found a chocolate bunny, a skipping rope and a new doll." She held out her new doll for Irene's inspection as Rachel exchanged smiles with Kyle. "Isn't she pretty, Grandma?"

"She's very pretty, Ava." Standing in the doorway separating the dining and living room, Irene bent, and cupped her granddaughter's face. "She has big blue eyes like you." As Ava beamed up at her grandma, Rachel noted the way Kyle's glance went to the picture of James on the table beside him. Irene clapped her hands, calling all their attention. "Now let's all get washed up. Dinner is ready."

Rachel pushed off the sofa, and sucked in a breath when

Kyle's troubled glance left the picture of James and settled on her. He studied her for a long moment, like he was trying to figure something out.

"Are you okay?" she asked.

He set down the tumbler of whisky he'd been nursing and stood. "Yeah, I...I don't know." He shook his head. "I think I'm tired."

"Ava wearing you out?"

He laughed. "Something like that."

With her doll in one hand, Ava grabbed Rachel's hand with the other and tugged. "Come on, Mommy. Grandma made turkey."

"How about we leave your doll in here."

She frowned and was about to protest when Rachel dropped to one knee. "We can tuck her into the chair here, and that way she won't get any of that yummy cranberry sauce on her."

Ava thought about it for a moment then nodded. She ran over to the chair that Kyle had been sitting on and set her down.

"Good girl." Rachel captured her hand. They stepped into the dining room to find the table beautifully set for Easter dinner. It was nice. So nice. Rachel longed for family events like this.

"This looks wonderful, Irene," she said.

"Thank you." Irene smiled, and gestured for everyone to sit.

"Uncle Kyle, sit by me," Ava said as she hopped into her chair.

Kyle sat beside her, and Rachel took the seat across from her daughter and next to Irene. She grabbed her napkin and shook it out as Reg sat at the head of the table, a smile on his face as he looked around at all his family members. His glance stopped on Rachel, and she took in the lines bracketing his eyes. He seemed different somehow, more relaxed. Did it have something to do with Kyle and their talk?

"Thank you for coming, Rachel," he said, a warmth and welcoming tone in his voice that she'd never heard before. It touched her, deeply.

She twisted the napkin in her hand. "I'm happy to be here," she said, barely able to get the words past the lump forming in her throat.

"That's just what I wanted to hear." He reached for the bowl of mashed potatoes. "Now let's eat."

Kyle grabbed the plate of turkey and held it while Ava used the fork to grab a slice. Then he helped her with the fixings. Rachel's heart swelled as she watched them. He was a good man, a great man, and she couldn't put off telling him any longer. Tonight, when dinner was over, and Ava was tucked in bed, they'd have to talk.

Ava chatted endlessly as they ate, talking about the tree house, her friend's puppy and Cuddles, otherwise known as Marley. Of course her grandparents had probably heard all of this yesterday when Kyle had taken her to the cottage for the afternoon.

"Ava, it sounds like you and Kyle are having a lot of fun," Irene said.

She nodded, her blonde curls bouncing around her shoulder. "Uncle Kyle cried yesterday," Ava said matter-of-factly as she put a fork full of potatoes in her mouth. She chewed, swallowed, and added, "Grandpa says I need a daddy. If Uncle Kyle were my daddy I could get a dog."

Rachel's fork fell from her hand and clattered on her plate. Beside her Irene stiffened, her hands going flat on the table.

"Ava, honey..." Rachel shook her head and pushed back in her chair.

Irene turned and glared at Rachel, her eyes shooting

daggers. "Don't you see what you're doing?" Irene said, the calmness in her voice belying the anger on her face.

"Mom," Kyle began, holding his hand up as he came to Rachel's defense. "Don't start—"

"All this playing house you're doing with my son is confusing Ava." Rachel's jaw dropped and Irene narrowed her eyes and continued. "It's also confusing Kyle. He's only home for a couple of weeks and look what you've done to him. He's falling into your—"

"Don't," Rachel warned. Rage moved though Rachel as she climbed to her feet. Kyle stood, sending his chair backward as he crossed the table to put his arm around her.

"Rach," he said, heat and strength radiating from him as he drew her close. "Let me handle this."

She shook her head to stop him. As a peacekeeper, she might have put up with a lot from Irene over the years, but the one thing she wouldn't put up with was her saying anything bad about Kyle—especially in front of Ava.

"We are not *playing* at anything. My feelings for Kyle are as real as they were for James. And I think James would be happy that both Ava and I have him in our life."

Kyle held her close, offering her his support, and when she looked up at this powerful military man—a man who upped and join the army, taking them all by surprise—understanding hit like a lightning bolt. Oh. My. God. There was so much more to this man than she knew. Not only was he power and strength, he was kind and compassionate. Everything he did —everything he'd given up, including her—was for his brother. Her heart swelled with love.

She swallowed past the tightness in her throat. "He's a good man, Irene. One of the best men I know. Just like James was." Irene might have hated Rachel, but there wasn't anything she wouldn't do for her family. She'd wanted only what was best for her boys and Rachel couldn't fault her for that. She too wanted what was best for Ava. "They became good men—kind, compassionate and putting the needs of others first—because of you. You did a good job raising them."

Irene's eyes went wide, and she sat there staring at Rachel, her mouth opening and closing like she had no idea what to say in retaliation. She climbed to her feet and stumbled slightly. She gripped the edge of the table to support herself. "I...I..."

"Enough," Reg bellowed. "That's enough, Irene."

Ava started crying, and it snapped Rachel back. She sucked in a quick breath. "Ava, honey." *Oh, God!* "It's okay."

"Mommy," she cried, holding her arms out. Rachel rushed to her daughter and lifted her from the chair. She turned and Kyle was right there, arms wide, ready to comfort and defend.

"I want to go." She ran her hands through Ava's hair and held her against her shoulder.

He nodded, put his arms around the two and led them to the front door. Without looking back, they left the house. Her body was still shaking when Kyle put them in the car. She sat in the backseat with Ava and talked quietly to her, explaining how sometimes adults didn't get along and none of it was her fault.

She kept stealing glances at Kyle, taking in the hard lines of his profile in the dashboard light. His hands gripped the wheel, and tension oozed off his body in waves. Twenty minutes later they pulled into her driveway and Ava started crying again.

She touched her daughter's face. "Sweetheart, it's okay."

"No, Mommy. I forgot my dolly."

Kyle put his arm on the seat and turned. His voice was soft when he said, "Why don't you two head on in. I'll go back and get it."

"Kyle," she began, shaking her head. The last thing he needed tonight was another confrontation with his parents.

"It's okay. Ava needs her doll."

Ava sniffed, and Kyle climbed from the car to open the back door. Rachel helped Ava from her seat and Kyle scooped her up and carried her up the stairs. Rachel opened the door and he stepped in behind her. He set Ava down and sank to one knee.

He brushed his thumb over her cheeks to dry her tears. "You go get washed up for bed, and I'll be right back, okay?"

She squeezed his face, kissed his nose, then darted up the stairs. He stood, and when sad eyes met hers, Rachel nearly sobbed all over again.

"You okay?" He cupped the back of her neck and drew her close.

She nodded. "You?"

He dipped his head. "Yeah." His lips met hers for a soft kiss full of emotion, tenderness. His hands went to her shoulders and he inched back. His eyes met hers and there was a note of desperation in his voice when he said "When I get back, we need to talk."

He was right, they did need to talk, and what she had to say would either bring them closer together or tear them wide apart.

K yle pulled into his parents' driveway and killed the ignition. He took a couple of deep breaths to pull himself together then made his way to the front door.

"Kyle," his father said, a new weariness in his eyes as he stood back and waved him in.

"I'm just here for Ava's doll."

"We need to talk."

"Actually, we don't."

"Your mother and I had a long talk after you left. I explained a lot of things."

"Did you explain that if she can't treat Rachel with respect then she can't expect to see me anymore?" He walked past his father and found Ava's doll on the recliner he'd been sitting in earlier.

"Kyle, I'm sorry," his mother's soft voice said from behind.

He spun, dropping the doll back in the chair. "For what? Accusing Rachel of trying to trick me in to playing house, or insinuating that I'm too stupid to see it?"

"You're far from stupid," she whispered, clasping and

unclasping her hands. Silence fell heavily for a moment. As tension filled the air, she took a tentative step toward him. "When she said I did a good job with you boys, I never...I never knew she felt that way."

"That's because you never gave her a chance. You saw what you wanted to see in her and never thought she was good enough." He ran his hands through his hair. "Wasn't the fact that James loved her enough for you to accept her, just the way she was?"

"You're right. It wasn't fair to James. It wasn't fair to Rachel. I've made so many mistakes. With Rachel, with James...with you. I see that now." Tears filled her eyes. "I don't want to lose you too, Kyle."

Kyle's heart pinched. "I'm your son, you're not going to lose me. But I love Rachel, Mom. I want to be with her, and I want to take care of Ava. You're going to have to accept that."

"I want you to be happy, Kyle. I've only ever wanted what was best for you and James."

Being with Ava and wanting what was best for her helped him understand where his mother was coming from. He didn't agree with her methods, but at least he could now understand how protective she was. A long, slow breath left his lungs as the fight went out of him.

"I know," he said quietly.

His dad put his hand on his shoulder. "Then go to them. They both love you, Kyle, and you'll be a great father to that little girl."

At the mention of *father*, a prickly sensation ran down the back of his neck. He picked up Ava's doll, his glance once again going to the picture of James. He straightened, his mind taking that moment to go back to when he'd found Ava's medical papers. That's when it hit him. James was a universal donor, yet Ava's blood type was rare, like his.

*She has your eyes.*

*Looks like you.*

Bile punched into his throat, and his legs nearly gave out. He'd had sex with Rachel nine months before she'd given birth to Ava. Jesus Christ! Jesus fucking Christ! He'd been so wrapped up in guilt he never stopped to consider she could be his. Then again, he and James had looked so much alike, he just assumed...

Blood drained to his toes as he picked the doll up with a shaky hand and turned. He needed answers and he needed them now.

"Kyle, what is it?" his father asked.

Kyle shook his head and rushed past him. "I have to go."

His parents were speaking, saying something, but he couldn't comprehend. His brain was spinning, his stomach clenching so hard it was all he could do not to vomit.

He jumped into Rachel's car and peeled out of the driveway. He rolled his window down, blasting himself with the cool evening air to get his head on straight. Maybe he was wrong. Maybe Ava had Rachel's blood type and he was simply reading more in to this than he should. Yeah, that had to be it. Surely to God if he was the child's father, Rachel would have told him. Keeping something like that a secret was unforgiveable in his book.

He raced toward her place, and even though there was a logical explanation to all this, he still couldn't dispel the unease pulling at him. He parked in her driveway, and with the front door key in hand, rushed up the steps.

The door clicked open and he found Rachel sitting at the foot of the stairs, like she'd been waiting for him. With tension in her body, her hands twisted the hem of her shirt, and a very bad feeling moved through him. A very bad feeling indeed.

"Rachel." His gaze moved over her face. One look at her

and he knew. "Oh, God, Rachel. Jesus Christ. She's mine, isn't she?"

Her hands wrapped around her stomach and she leaned forward, hugging herself. "I wanted to tell you." Her voice was so low he had to strain to hear.

His knees nearly went out from underneath him. He leaned against the door for support, trying to process, to wrap his brain around this unexpected turn of events.

"Why didn't you tell me?" He shook his head, every emotion from fear, anger, love, and happiness hitting at the same time. "Why would you keep something like this from me?"

Her face paled. "I didn't want you to hate me, or hate yourself any more than you already do."

Holy Christ. His betrayal to his brother went way deeper than he even realized. "Fuck." He grabbed a fistful of hair. This was bad, so fucking bad.

"I thought if you loved me before I told you, it might make it easier."

"Love you?" A need he couldn't suppress blew through him like a grenade. He loved her. He'd always loved her. So fucking much that he had to run halfway across the world after she'd married James. "You wanted me to love you? Rachel, I've always loved you. Always. From the minute I first met you I loved you. That's why I had to leave. I couldn't stay here and watch you with James, even though I knew it was the best thing for you."

"You didn't know it, you thought it." Tears rolled down her cheek. "And I always loved you too, Kyle."

"No, you loved James. You two belonged together."

"I did love James, but I loved you too." She blinked up at him, a mix of hope and fear dancing in her eyes. "And maybe you and I were the ones who belonged together. I know we would have made choices that were right for both of us."

"Don't say that," he shot back. But on some level he couldn't help but think she was right. She had loved James, but her years with him hadn't been happy ones. He could see that now.

"I didn't want to go back to him, Kyle. It really was over between us. But you made it clear you didn't want me, that I belonged with James. I accepted that because I truly did love him too. He promised he'd stopped letting his mother run our lives and I gave him another chance, hoping he'd be true to his word and we would be happy." She stood and took a step toward him. "I know you hate yourself for what we did that day. I agree, the timing wasn't right. I'd just broken it off with James. But what we did, and the child we created, doesn't feel wrong in my heart."

"I leave in three days. Were you just going to let me go without telling me?"

"I wanted to tell you. I was scared. I...what if you didn't want us...what if you left? And I didn't want you to stay because of obligation. I wanted you to stay because you wanted to, because you wanted *us*."

He pushed off the door. "I can't believe this, Rachel. I deserved to know long before this."

"I only found out when she was tested."

"You should have told me then." He gripped the door handle so hard, his knuckles turned white. Needing air to clear his head and help get it on straight, he yanked on it.

She moved toward him, and her hand landed on his arm. "Wait."

He hissed in air as she touched him. Blood pounded through his veins, and it became harder and harder to breathe. He turned to her. "You should have told me."

She backed up and her tears fell harder. "I'm so sorry, Kyle. I'm so sorry. But please don't leave. Let's talk."

"I can't." He scrubbed his chin and clenched down on his jaw. "I'm not sure what I'll even say to you."

"I can't take you leaving again. It broke my heart in two. If you go now, it will shatter me and I might not be able to let you back in."

With her words ringing in his ears, he walked out the door and pulled it shut. As it closed behind him, a breeze washed over his face, stinging like a hard slap. Feeling numb inside, completely off kilter, he climbed into Jack's truck.

*Ava was his daughter.*

He pounded on the steering wheel. He'd done his brother wrong, so fucking wrong. He drove aimlessly for hours, then made his way to James's burial site. Day bled to night as he strolled through the cemetery, until he came to James's resting place.

He ran his hand over the marble tombstone and sank to his knees.

"I'm so sorry," he said, unable to hold the tears back. "I'm so goddamn sorry." He stayed like that until the night air grew cool and other visitors left to go back to their surviving loved ones. All went quiet around him, save for the crickets and a few animals scurrying about. He lowered his head and stared at the ground, seconds turning to minutes. Minutes turning to hours.

"I thought I might find you here." The comment came from behind.

At the sound of his father's voice he swiped at his cheeks and worked to pull himself together. "I didn't know you were looking for me," he managed to get out.

"Something happened tonight at the house. You ran out of the place like you'd seen a ghost. I drove by Rachel's and when I didn't see the truck, I thought I'd check the next logical place."

"And you found me."

His father stepped closer. "Do you want to tell me what happened?"

He exhaled slowly. No sense in hiding the truth any more. He planned to stay and do the right thing and soon enough everyone would know.

"Ava's mine. She's my child. My daughter." Tears fell once again, soaking the grass at his knees. "Years ago before the wedding, Rachel gave the ring back and came looking for me. I made a terrible mistake that day. Much worse than I ever knew." His father went quiet for a long, long time, as Kyle stared at the headstone through blurry eyes. "How could she have kept this from me?"

"Probably because she was afraid you'd hate her, and yourself."

"James didn't deserve this from me. He was a good brother, a good husband."

His father put his hand on Kyle's shoulder. "Do you believe in fate, son?"

"I don't know."

"Sometimes things happen that we have no control over."

"Maybe, but what I did was wrong."

"You were loyal to your brother, maybe more loyal than he deserved, but Ava was made out of love, not betrayal. I know that. From the bottom of my heart, I know that, Kyle."

"I've always loved Rachel," he said in a quiet voice. How could he not, she was so easy to love, so easy to be with. She was everything to him.

"James knew it too."

His heart missed a beat as he looked over his shoulder at his father. "What are you talking about?"

"He knew you loved her, and he wanted her for himself, which was why he jumped on her first. He didn't put your needs first."

"Don't." He gave a hard shake of his head. "Don't you say anything bad about him."

"I'm only speaking the truth. He was my son and I loved him. But what I'm trying to say is he's not perfect and neither are you. We all make mistakes."

"He was perfect, Dad. I made sure of it."

"I know you did. But James's death changed me, made me see the world differently. Made me realize just how unhappy Rachel had been. She loved him and would do anything for him—like ignore what she really wanted and move into a big mansion with him. But none of those things made her happy. She sacrificed a lot to be with James, and you sacrificed your entire life for him."

"He taught me to read, to tie my shoes, to kill the monsters in the closet. He stood up for me on the playground. He gave me his Popsicle when mine fell. He looked out for me. When he needed your approval, all I did was make sure he got it."

"You're a good solider and a good brother, always going above and beyond. But maybe it's time for you to jump on what you want and find the happiness you and Rachel both deserve." His father dropped down beside him.

"Dad..." The cords in his neck were strung so tight it was hard to talk.

"It's time to let go of the past. You need to forgive Rachel and yourself."

"I forgive her." He took a deep breath and let it out. "She never meant to hurt me."

"Just like you never meant to hurt your brother. He knows that, Kyle."

Kyle lifted his head and met his father's weary eyes. "Yeah?"

His father nodded. "He'd want you to be happy, and he'd want Rachel and Ava taken care of."

"You think so?"

"Yes. So what will make you happy, son?"

"Taking care of Rachel and Ava."

"Then what are you still doing here?"

He fisted his hands and pounded them together. "I ran out on her. I fucking ran out when she told me. She said she couldn't handle me running out on her again, and I did it anyways. I am such an asshole."

"You needed time to think. But now that you've had time to figure out what you want, you need to go back, and make this right. I want my family back, son."

"What if I'm too late?"

"What if you're not?"

He sniffed and wiped his face with the back of his hand. Joints cracking from sitting on his knees so long, he climbed to his feet and turned to his father. "Thank you." He held his arms out and his father pulled him in for a hug.

He pulled back and turned Kyle toward his truck. "Go get her. Go get your family."

With renewed purpose, he hurried to his truck. It was late, but before he went to her, there was one stop he needed to make first. One girl that could very well help him get back into Rachel and Ava's life.

Close to an hour later he parked his truck on the street, and glanced at Rachel's house. All the lights were off. Shit, what if she wouldn't let him in, or worse, had taken off to someplace where he could never find them. He still had his key, and would use it if he had to, but he'd prefer it if Rachel welcomed him back in. He looked at the girl sitting beside him.

"I'll be right back, okay?" She turned from him and stared at the dark house, shifting anxiously like she could feel Kyle's tension.

He walked along her driveway, but a noise at the back of

the house, a half cry, half hiccup sound caught his attention. He picked up the pace and darted around the back. The light outside the back door was on and he looked up at the deck to find it empty, then he darted a glance around the semi-lit yard.

The noise sounded again and he turned toward the tree house. The light fanning out in the yard reached the small door he'd built for Ava. Rachel. Jesus Christ. She was in the tree house, and she was crying.

"Rach," he said quietly, and the noise stopped abruptly. Three steps took him to the towering tree and he braced his hands on the tree house door, glancing inside as his eyes adjusted to the darkness. "Hey," he whispered.

"Hey."

"Can I come in?"

She sniffed. "No."

His heart crashed against his ribcage. "Rach, come on. Please let me come in."

"What do you want?"

"I want to talk." She went quiet and he said, "Please. You don't have to say anything. Just listen, okay?"

A beat and then, "Fine."

He listened to her clothes rustle as she moved over to make room for him. Hoisting himself up, he pushed through the opening and sat beside her. He mimicked her position by bending his legs and resting his elbows on his knees. They sat in silence for a long time, the sounds on the streets and a dog barking a few houses away breaking the uneasy quiet.

"I'm kind of a dick," he said, cutting through the tension between them.

A noise crawled out of her throat and he couldn't tell whether it was a laugh, hiccup, or cry. She stayed quiet, and he just listened to them breathe as their bodies touched.

When she finally spoke she came back with, "If you're waiting for me to voice an argument, I'm not going to."

"That's because you're kind of a dick too."

"I am not." She whacked him. He feigned hurt, but it filled his heart...reminded him of old times.

"Actually, you kind of are." He angled his head her way and playfully nudged her with his shoulder. "You know, for not telling me I had a daughter and all."

A breath shuddered past her lips and washed over his face. "Kyle—"

"But you know what. We're both dicks, and it doesn't matter." He shifted his body, turning to face her as he crossed his legs. "Because I love you, Rach. I love you so fucking much. I'm so sorry I left when you needed me to stay." He reached out and pulled one of her hands into his lap. "Not just tonight but four years ago, and again after James's death. I don't want to live without you and Ava in my life. I love you, Rachel. I love Ava. Please tell me I didn't fuck this all up for us. And if I did, tell me how to make it right. I'm not leaving here," he pointed down, toward the tree house floor. "I'm not leaving this spot until you tell me I can stay, because every reason I have for staying is here, right in front of me."

She straightened her legs and when she glanced past his shoulder, toward the tree house opening, his entire body stiffened. Was she leaving? Jesus Christ, he couldn't handle it if she turned her back on him the way he had with her so many times.

But then she crossed her legs and faced him. Her palms went to his face, and she squeezed, squishing his cheeks, a gesture that reminded him so much of his daughter.

*His daughter...*

Ava was his little girl and that made him the luckiest fucking man alive. He didn't even want to take another breath without her being in his life, squishing his face, laughing when he called her squirt, and teaching her life skills.

"Kyle," Rachel said softly. "I think you need to stop hanging around Ava."

His heart stopped, air leaving his lungs in a whoosh. As worry flooded him, his throat squeezed and tears pricked his eyes. This couldn't be happening. "Rachel, please..." he began, choking on his words.

"You're starting to talk too much, just like her." The smile tugging at her mouth helped restart his heart.

He leaned in, pressed his forehead to hers and cupped the back of her neck. "Rach," he murmured, brushing his lips over hers as oxygen refilled his lungs. "You scared me."

"You scared me too. When you left, I never thought I'd see you again."

"I love you so much. I want to stay. I want to go back to school, get a degree, go work in my dad's office." He took a breath and let it out slowly. "I want to be your husband, Ava's daddy. I want to be a real family. Rachel, without you two, I'm nothing."

She started to cry again, and he brushed the tears away with his thumb. "Hey," he whispered. "What's wrong?"

"I want all that too, Kyle. I'm just so happy. Ava will be so happy."

"Come here," he pulled her to his lap and held her, memories of that day at the bluff no longer strangling him. They held each other for a long time, exchanging kisses as joyful tears ran down their faces. He inched away, wiped his cheeks, then hers. "Can we go tell her?"

She nodded. "There's nothing I'd rather do."

"Before we do, I need to talk to you about something else."

"What is it?"

"How about I show you instead."

"Kyle—"

"Come on." He climbed out of the tree house and held his hand out to help Rachel. Taking her hand in his and pulling her tight against him, he walked her to the front of her house and led her to the truck. He opened the passenger door and Rachel yelped when Cuddles, aka Marley, jumped out and started running circles around her.

"Kyle," she shrieked. "What's going on?"

"Meet Cuddles," he said.

She shook her head, but he captured her hands. "Just hear me out. I know you work full time, but if I go back to school so I can join Dad then I'll have odd hours and can take care of her."

"You're going to work at your dad's firm?"

He shrugged. "Yeah, I kind of always wanted to."

"I know," she said.

"You did?"

"Yeah, I did."

"And when I eventually go to work full time we can look at doggy day care."

She stared up at him, her eyes wide. "I can't believe this."

"Please say yes. I want to do this for Ava. We'll take care of her while you're at work I promise." He laughed. Jesus, he was actually starting to sound like Ava.

"Actually, I've been thinking."

"About?"

"Working part-time hours. With the office moving, I hate the idea of the longer commute. But that's not the entire reason. I've always worked hard for everything. I never wanted your mother to think I was a gold digger. But you know what, that doesn't matter anymore. I don't need to prove myself to anyone, least of all someone who has no respect for me."

He kissed her. "That's all going to change."

A little surprised look came over her face. "Oh, what makes you say that?"

"You stood up for yourself and me tonight. You did it with style and respect, Rach. You threw Mom for a loop, and opened her eyes in a lot of ways." He squeezed her hand. "Everything is changing, and we're going to be a family."

Tears pooled in her eyes again, and he hugged her because there was no one in the world who needed or deserved a family more than Rachel. Cuddles barked and they both glanced down at her.

"She's so big." Rachel laughed. "I think we might need a bigger house."

"Whatever you want, Rach. Always."

She smiled up at him, went up on her toes and pressed her lips to his. "You. What I want is you. All of you."

"So you keep saying." He grinned, and added, "But give it a month or two after I keep leaving the toilet seat up."

She pursed her lips and tapped her chin. "Hmm, come to think of it—"

"Hey," he said laughing. "Let's go." He looked at Cuddles and tapped his leg. "There's a little girl that's going to be very excited to see you." The dog's tail wagged harder, like she knew what he was saying.

Hand in hand, he and Rachel headed to the house, and Cuddles ran ahead like she couldn't wait to get there. He opened the door and Cuddles bolted through the main level sniffing everything. "Come on, girl."

They headed upstairs, and quietly opened Ava's door, blocking it slightly so Cuddles couldn't barge in and scare her.

"Ava," he whispered. "Are you awake?" Light from the hall spilled in to the room as Ava sat up and rubbed her eyes.

"Mommy?"

"I'm here," Rachel said.

Rachel walked in and sat on the edge of the bed. "Uncle Kyle has a surprise for you."

"Hey, Ava," he said quietly from the doorway.

She blinked as Cuddles banged against the door trying to get in.

"A surprise?"

He opened the door and Cuddles took off running toward her. Her eyes went wide, and she screamed, "Cuddles!"

The dog jumped on the bed and started licking her face, and she giggled hard. Kyle crossed the room, and eased Cuddles off her.

"Mommy, Mommy can I keep her?"

Kyle lowered himself onto her mattress as Cuddles jumped from the bed and ran around the room sniffing everything. Kyle took her little hand in his.

"So, Ava, we were thinking maybe I could be your daddy, and we could keep Cuddles. Would you like that?"

"You're going to be my daddy?"

"Yeah, I'm going to be your daddy, Ava." She squished his face, looked at Rachel, then back at him. "Did Mommy say it was okay?"

They both laughed hard. "Mommy says it's okay," Rachel said.

Ava kissed his nose. "Daddy," she squealed.

The weight behind that one word as it left her mouth was like a healing balm and helped put the last pieces of his heart back together.

Kyle looked at the two most important people in the world to him, and his heart swelled with all the love they offered him. He would love his brother forever, and always feel his absence, but it was time to let go of the guilt and be the man everyone needed him to be—including James.

# AFTERWORD

Thank you so much for reading, HIS REASON TO STAY, in my Line of Duty series. I hope you enjoyed the story! Be sure to check out the other 6 books in the series. Please keep reading for an excerpt of YOURS TO TAKE.

- His Obsession Next Door
- His Strings to Pull (Novella)
- His Trouble in Tallulah
- His Taste of Temptation
- His Moment to Steal
- His Best Friend's Girl
- His Reason to Stay

Interested in leaving a review? Please do! Reviews help readers connect with books that work for them. I appreciate all reviews, whether positive or negative.

Happy Reading,
  *Cathryn*

## YOURS TO TAKE

"Please tell me you're not serious?"

Jaw slack, and hands planted on the small round table, Rebecca Andrews stared at her three best friends, hardly able to believe what they were suggesting.

Lilliana James closed her palm over Rebecca's hand and gave a reassuring squeeze. Even though the lights had been dimmed in their favorite New York piano bar, a place where they all convened after a challenging day in the courtroom, Rebecca didn't miss the sympathy in her friend's big brown eyes when she said, "Come on, Becs, you know as well as I do that you need a vacation."

"It's not a vacation she needs," Melanie Collins piped in, running her fingers up and down the crystal stemware in a highly suggestive manner that had Rebecca's thoughts careening in an erotic direction. She smirked and added, "What she needs is to get laid. Plain and simple."

"Good, God," Rebecca murmured under her breath, hoping like hell no one in the near vicinity could hear her tell-it-like-it-is friend.

"Don't even try to deny it," Melanie challenged playfully, her eyes gleaming with mischief.

As their conversation headed south—literally—Rebecca fished her olive out of the martini glass and gestured the bartender for another, having decided then and there that this was the perfect occasion to overturn her two two-drink rule. Hell, who could blame her for wanting to consume copious amounts of alcohol after discovering her well-meaning friends wanted to send her to some sort of sex club on a private island off the coast of Nova Scotia?

She chewed on her olive as her glance went to the tickets on the table—one for a resort called Freedom, the other for the private charter that was scheduled to fly her there first thing tomorrow. Groaning, she took in the other patrons seated around them, many of whom were colleagues, their identities masked by the lounge's dark lighting and intimate seating. She leaned forward, desperate to keep this embarrassing conversation private, and arched an accusing brow. "How long have you three been scheming this up, anyway?"

"Just a few weeks now," Melanie answered.

Rebecca did the mental math, her thoughts rewinding to three weeks ago, then shook her head, suddenly understanding what this was really all about. "Look, Jon didn't break up with me. I broke up with him." When her rebuttal was met with silence, she desperately searched for an alliance in the group. Her glance met Sophie's and she cast her a pleading look.

But Sophie simply shrugged and said, "Just like you broke up with Justin, Matthew, Phillip..."

"And we know, we know," Melanie said, rolling her eyes. "You just weren't compatible."

Rebecca held her hands up, palms out. "Okay, fine. I get it. You're saying I'm too picky." She frowned, and added, "It's just that...well, we weren't...they weren't," she paused, unable to put in to words what she truly felt. How could she explain what was missing from those relationships, when she couldn't identify it herself?

She took a moment to consider the men from her past. Not only were they successful, kind and generous, they were also deeply considerate lovers. A woman in her right mind would jump at the chance to date any one of those men. She sighed inwardly. Okay, perhaps the problem really did lie with her, and *she* was the one who wasn't in her right mind. But she just couldn't seem to find a man that suited her.

If only she could figure out what it was that was lacking...

Oddly enough her thoughts drifted back to last year's trial against Montgomery Charters, specifically to Quinn Montgomery, owner of the airline, and one of the world's youngest, self-made millionaires. Rebecca always prided herself on being calm, cool and collected, inside the courtroom and out, but there was just something about that man's steely command that threw her off her game. Whenever she met those intense black eyes from across the table, eyes that looked like they could see into the depth of her soul, something always compelled her to shy away. She wasn't sure what it was about the powerful tycoon that had her reacting in such a peculiar way, she only knew that he had the ability to rattle her hard-earned control, and because of it, she needed to keep her distance.

The bartender stepped up to the table with fresh drinks, and as his presence pulled her thoughts back to the conversation at hand, Rebecca shook her head, wondering why she was thinking of the powerful and enigmatic Quinn Montgomery after all this time.

Perhaps it was the fact that her friends had booked her flight through his airline...or perhaps it was something else entirely. Either way, he was a man she never wanted to come up against again, because the next time she wasn't so sure she could keep her composure.

"It's just a weekend away to relax, let you hair down." Melanie waved a dismissive hand like what they were suggesting was nothing more than an innocent day at the spa. Except what they wanted her to do had sex, sin and seduction written all over it. "Maybe at Freedom you'll learn to relax and stop trying to be in control of everything all the time."

Rebecca squared her shoulders and tucked a long, loose strand of hair back into the bun piled at the top of her head. "Hey, I don't always have to be in control of everything."

Her rebuttal was met with laughter. Okay, so maybe it was true, but it wasn't her fault. She'd come from nothing and had to work hard to get where she was, and it wasn't easy to loosen up and let go. Controlling every aspect of her life was how she got to where she was today.

*And where is that*, some inner voice asked, only to answer with, *alone every night, with nothing but a battery-operated friend to keep you warm*.

Sophie squeezed her hand and Rebecca looked up to meet a pair of big blue eyes full of genuine concern. "You've been so uptight that we just thought you could use a bit of time to yourself."

Melanie bobbed her head. "And you never know, while you're away maybe you'll figure out what it is you're looking for in a man."

"At a sex resort?"

"It's not a sex resort," Lilliana reassured her. "It's just a place where single people go to meet others."

Slipping into lawyer mode, Rebecca challenged, "But when you say *others*, you mean the opposite sex right? So in my book that's a sex resort." Rebecca picked up the ticket and turned it over in her hand, but as she thought about it, really, really thought about what her friend's were offering her, her body began warming in the most intimate places. She wet her suddenly dry lips, her nipples tightening as she envisioned the salacious activities that undoubtedly took place on the exclusive island.

A strange garbled noise caught in her throat and she shook her head to clear it. God, she must be crazy—and the jury was still out on that—because for a moment there she actually found herself considering their ludicrous offer.

Rebecca squinted to read the fine print. "Is this place even legal?"

"Of course it is, and you leave first thing in the morning." Melanie snatched the ticket and shoved it into Rebecca's purse; her way of saying the topic was no longer up for debate.

Rebecca stiffened. "I don't think—"

"Which is why we're doing the thinking for you," Lillian countered.

"If you're not at the airport by nine sharp, I'll personally drag you from your bed and take you there." Melanie finished her drink, and grinned. "And don't come back until you've had at least a dozen orgasms."

"And we don't want to hear a peep from you until Monday morning, when we'll meet you at the office to hear all the juicy details," Lilliana said. "If you call before then, we won't answer."

"That's right," Sophie added, pointing to Rebecca's purse. "You've just been gifted with a ticked to Freedom. So go. Be free."

---

Quinn Montgomery took one look at the flight manifest and felt his cock swell with an excitement he hadn't felt in a long time. As the Dom in him stirred to life, he carefully set the paper on his desk and took two measured steps to his office window. He adjusted his tie and blinked against the bright morning rays glistening on the wings of the Cessna idling quietly on the tarmac below. He turned his attention to his ground crew, who were performing maintenance checks before today's scheduled flights, but his thoughts were too preoccupied with the names on his manifest, one name in particular, to follow their progress.

*Rebecca Andrews.*

Now what were the odds that the lawyer who'd cost his company hundreds of thousands of dollars had booked a charter on one of his crafts? A charter to a hedonistic resort, nonetheless.

His mind raced back to last year's trial, and to the lawsuit Ms. Andrews' client never should have won. How it was his company's fault that Ms. Andrews' client had booked a package though a shady travel agent, only to find herself alone and stranded on Nantucket Island during one of the year's worst storm was beyond him. Yet in the end, his company had to go good for the damages, as well as the mental stress and loss of wages that the woman had allegedly suffered.

Quinn's mouth twitched and he scrubbed his hand over his chin as he rolled back and forth on the balls of his feet. While the money was only a drop in the bucket for his company, the tricks the lawyer had used to get what she wanted from him, left him wanting to use a few tricks of his own—to get what he wanted from her.

Oh yeah, watching her from the hot seat during his trial, watching that sharp tongue of hers in action, had him wanting to find other ways to put that smart mouth of hers to work. Heat prowled through his body as he thought about how Ms. Andrews kept her control close, kept her body poised and her head held high. But during the proceeding, every time her glance had landed on him and she lowered her gaze in a submissive move, he knew she was in denial. Damned if he didn't want to be the one to open her eyes and her body, and put her in touch with her deeper needs.

Even though they'd never crossed paths since the trial, she'd consumed his thoughts for well over a year now. He'd spent many nights thinking about the ways he'd like to strip her bare and give her ass a good hard paddling for wrongfully stealing money from his company. But the truth was, what he wanted had little to do with revenge, and more to do with showing the woman who dressed in prim and proper business suits that real control came in the form of surrender.

With his cock throbbing, and heat coursing through him, he moved back to his desk to look over the day's schedule a second time. He glanced at her name again, and his entire body came alive, because there was no denying that he'd just been gifted the perfect opportunity to help her free her submissive side. Of course, given that he'd only have one weekend, he'd have no choice but to push her limits and resort to some stronger methods to seduce the submission out of her. His fingers itched as he thought about that lush heart-shaped ass of hers and how much it needed his attention.

He inspected the itinerary closer and discovered that Jack Armstrong, a pilot that had been with the company since its early days was scheduled to depart for Freedom at nine sharp —Ms. Andrews the only passenger on board. Quinn considered her final destination. Not only had his company taken guests to the private island numerous time, he personally knew the resort well, having played there a time or two. Although this time he suspected the plane wasn't going to make it to the well-known island nestled in the Atlantic Ocean, especially if he was the one in the pilot seat.

He picked up the paper, and traced his finger over her

name as a devious plan began to formulate in his mind. As he sorted through all the naughty details, all the tricks he was going to use on her, he checked his watch then picked up his phone to call his personal assistant. After giving her a list of things he needed before takeoff, he dialed a friend and called in a favor. Once all the pieces were in place, and the discreet information he needed was on its way, he crossed Jack's name off the manifesto, shrugged out of his dress jacket and grabbed his flight suit. Ms. Andrews might be looking for a little adventure at Freedom, but he'd be damned if he wasn't going to be the guy to give her what she really wanted, yet had no idea how much she needed.

# ABOUT CATHRYN

*New York Times* and *USA today* Bestselling author, Cathryn is a wife, mom, sister, daughter, and friend. She loves dogs, sunny weather, anything chocolate (she never says no to a brownie) pizza and red wine. She has two teenagers who keep her busy with their never ending activities, and a husband who is convinced he can turn her into a mixed martial arts fan. Cathryn can never find balance in her life, is always trying to find time to go to the gym, can never keep up with emails, Facebook or Twitter and tries to write page-turning books that her readers will love.

Connect with Cathryn:
Newsletter
https://app.mailerlite.com/webforms/landing/c1f8n1
Twitter: https://twitter.com/writercatfox
Facebook:
https://www.facebook.com/AuthorCathrynFox?ref=hl
Blog: http://cathrynfox.com/blog/
Goodreads:
https://www.goodreads.com/author/show/91799.Cathryn_Fox

Pinterest http://www.pinterest.com/catkalen/

Hands On

Body Contact

Full Exposure

Dossier

Private Reserve

House Rules

Under Pressure

Big Catch

Brazilian Fantasy

Improper Proposal

Boys of Beachville

Good at Being Bad

Igniting the Bad Boy

Bad Girl Therapy

Stone Cliff Series:

Crashing Down

Wasted Summer

Love Lessons

Wrapped Up

Eternal Pleasure Series

Instinctive

Impulsive

Indulgent

Sun Stroked Series

Seaside Seduction

**Deep Desire**

**Private Pleasure**

**Captured and Claimed Series:**

Yours to Take

Yours to Teach

Yours to Keep

**Firefighter Heat Series**

Fever

Siren

Flash Fire

**Playing For Keeps Series**

Slow Ride

Wild Ride

Sweet Ride

**Breaking the Rules:**

Hold Me Down Hard

Pin Me Up Proper

Tie Me Down Tight

**Stand Alone Title:**

Hands on with the CEO

Torn Between Two Brothers

Holiday Spirit

Unleashed

Knocking on Demon's Door

Web of Desire

www.ingramcontent.com/pod-product-compliance
Lightning Source LLC
Chambersburg PA
CBHW050403190726
48284CB00007BB/2406